Coming Full Circle

Jrayis Deyond

To: Le'sh Anne
From Jrayis Deyond
Thank you to i the love & support
8-24-19
J. Thomas

Thanks to:

To my Creator

Mokha Kentwood & STORY POET for the Cover Art Work

My Family

Thank you for your love and support.

To everybody who got this book. Dare to Dream then Live your Dream

Love Always,

Jerrick Thomas

Jrayis Deyond

Chapter 1

Well today was my college graduation, 4 years' undergrad in Journalism and 2 years in Theater Arts had come to a close. I got my degrees and I was making plans to move back home to Shreveport, Louisiana from Michigan that week to be close to my sister and our family back home.

Once my flight landed at the airport, my sister, Lucy was there saying she had a surprise for me. On the ride home we talked and got caught up on the last 6 years of me being MIA. At her place she was telling me all about the apartment she had arranged for me right down the street.

We went down to check this place out. We headed out to Summit Villa and rode through the city to see how much things have changed with shopping centers and the city seemed to be flourishing since I went away to Michigan State years ago. The manager Shelia was expecting us.

We went and looked at the place and it was quite nice. 1 bedroom with a walk-in closet, nice kitchen and dining area and the bathroom was very nice as well, with a shower which I loved and not to mention the apartment would be ready in a few days, giving me time for my furniture and things to come in.

I put down the deposit and explained I'd move in as soon as my furniture came in, lucky for me I had some cash saved from working while I was in school to tie me over until I had a found a job and get back on my feet.

Back at Lucy's she had started a family, had married her childhood sweetheart LaDorian Long and was expecting her first child in a few months. She had a guestroom all set up for me while I waited for my things to arrive.

I had applied for a job at The Times newspaper here in town and was meeting with Mrs. Lee the director tomorrow, which gave me time to get out and see my hometown and catch up with everything going on in the city.

Today was crazy, Lucy told me that Lena had called for me, Lena was an old friend from high school, and I got the number from Lucy and called her to catch up.

The phone rang a few times and she finally answered

 "Hello dearie"

 "Hey Ji how you been?"

 "Well I'm good just finished with school, just got home this morning, and been cooling since I got back, how have you been doing honey?"

"Well my son, Kenny is 4 years old now, oh and I saw you're boo too!" she said while laughing.

"Who is that sweetie, when I just got back in town this morning?"

"You're Jeffery, your baby, remember, oh it's been a while hasn't it lol?"

"How are things with you?" Trying to change the subject

"Good, I'm good I have to work tonight."

"Well, I'm going out tonight, it's been a while, since I've just gone out and let my hair down, maybe we can catch up sometime soon honey."

Later that evening, I woke up from my nap and got dressed and was on my way out the door at 11:30 for Calintes. I paid the doorman and went inside to grab myself a table right outside of the dance floor.

I was sitting there watching the crowd, having a drink and having a great time.

As the night went on I couldn't help but to notice this guy, I knew him from high school, he was 6'1, dark brown skin, dark brown eyes, with a low haircut and nice smile.

He came over.

"Jisain Styles main, you don't remember me, Tyson Jacks, we had English IV, I sat like 4 seats behind you, and you never noticed me because I was a little shy."

"Well looks like you've opened up a lot old friend, have a seat Ty, I can call you Ty right?" me flirting.

"Tell me something, what really sent you over to my table?" I asked sounding intrigued.

"Just to talk, that's all really catch up with you, to see how to make you mine."

"Ok what's it been like 7, 8 years or something and who's to say that I never paid you any attention. I kept an eye on you, you just didn't catch me that was all and what do you mean make you mine?" I asked him softly.

"How about I get your number and I call you tonight, we can talk?"

"Alright you got me, you're playing right, you want my number, you?" I was joking.

"Well here is my cell 208-4704," he said, I called the number and his phone began to ring.

"So the phone number is real, the question is, are you?"

"I could use a blunt."

"Oh you smoke."

"Yes I smoke, I've been smoking for years since high school, and I would come to class so stoned."

"So let's go smoke one now," He said perking up.

"Not with you Sweetie, but I'll call you, I have to go".

As I got up from the table, he was following right behind.

"Can I walk you to your car?"

"That's cool."

As we made our way out to my car, I was so anxious, I opened the door, sat inside and went to close the door, when he stood there inside the door, smiling big as ever.

"I will be waiting for your call tonight."

"You just are up, well I'm headed to IHOP, and it's time for breakfast, would you like to go?" Me being generous to offer

"Yeah sure I'll go, if you'll bring me back?"

"Yeah I'll bring you back."

In the car, I was very curious about what was taking place. This man from school was here with me ready to take the time to get to know me.

At IHOP we sat and talked. Tyson was telling me all about him knowing when he was gay.

It was during middle school, he would have these dreams that were weird, but he kept it all to himself.

"Then that day, you walked into class you're first day at Byrd, you stood up and introduced yourself, I liked your brown eyes and that cute ass smile, I was intrigued by you and I just knew I wanted you."

"So for what seven, eight years or so you've been gay, I know you've been dating?"

"I can say I've had my share but I'm still looking for love."

It was dawn and I needed to be headed home, interview was in a few hours, so we paid our bills for breakfast and we were off to Tyson's car at the club where he left it. We made our way back to the parking lot, we pulled up to his car, I gave him a hug and that was that.

I briefly arrived back to Lucy's house around 3:30 am, I creped inside to not disturb them, when I received a message from Tyson, he had made it home safe.

I said a prayer and I was off to bed.

Chapter 2

The interview was a success. I got the job with The Times newspaper, Mrs. Lee was very impressed me. She liked my resume, my references, was very impressed with me, she highly recommended me for the job and the interview was outstanding.

She told me I started in a few days once things were set with the office space for me.

After the interview, I took a drive over to Greenwood Cemetery to see my mom and dad. They had died many years ago.

The story is they were driving back home from a party in Houston, heading back the car stopped on the freeway, the gas station wasn't that far, so my dad Keith Lemont Styles II went off to get gas, my mother Diana Lillyanna Styles stayed behind with the car. Dad was robbed and shot and my mom raped and strangled, their bodies were discovered after weeks of searching for them and that was that. Lucy and I were sent to Shreveport to live with our Uncle Joey, daddy's brother.

At their graves, I told them all about my job, how I had finished school and getting my degrees and that Lucy was married and about to have her baby a girl, to be named Mariah. The tears begin to fall down my cheek, when I was thinking about how proud they would be of me and Lucy, seeing us doing so wonderful with our lives.

I made my way back to the car, where I could hear the phone buzzing, it was Tyson.

"Hello."

"Hey, what's up bro, why you sound so sad?"

"Oh coming from visiting my parents grave site that all."

"Oh I'm sorry about that."

"You didn't know, so what are you doing this afternoon?" I asked trying to cheer up.

"I'm good man, just laying here blowing one in the wind, that's all really, thought about you and I said I'd give you a call."

"Oh okay I just had an interview at The Times newspaper, this morning, I got the job was about to head back to my sister's Lucy, place before the movers bring in my things in from Michigan today."

"I was thinking maybe we could link up and chill."

"Yeah sure, I can do that."

"Ok I'll text you my address and you can come by my place later this evening."

"I live in Fox Creek off Mansfield Road just, hit me up and I'll meet you out-front tonight."

I got back to Lucy's and shared the news with her about the job and that I'd be moving out that day, because the movers were coming in with my things for the apartment.

Around 3, the movers had finally came in with my things, I met with them at the apartment to help them unload the truck, Lucy and

LaDorian came over to help me with unpacking the truck. We set up the furniture and carried the boxes inside to be unpacked. For the next few hours I spent the day making sure things were decent and in order, the way I wanted it.

I dropped off them, and drove over to meet up with Tyson. I called him and let him know I was on my way.

"I'm on the way to your place."

"Oh okay, I'll be out-front when you get here."

"Yeah I'm on the freeway, I'll be there shortly, and I'll be looking for you."

I pulled into the parking lot and there he was waiting, in his car waiting for me to follow him to his place. We parked the cars and walked up to his door. When he opened the door, we walked inside.

Damn nice place, grown and sexy, was the thought running across my mind.

We settled in on the couch while Tyson rolled up some herb for us to smoke.

I asked himself all about himself and his last relationship. Tyson was 27 years old, he's a Virgo, he has been working as a construction worker since high school and he loved his job. He dated his ex for 6 years and he told me how had broking up.

The guy was cool and things were good for a long time they were in love. Then for the last 2 years of the relationship the guy began to accuse him of cheating. Tyson would find hickeys on his body, the guy would pick fights, and he really just changed.

He said he was fed up and he set him up. He said he went off to work one morning, which was a friend's house. He had asked his friend drop him off at his apartment, when he arrived home there was a car parked in his parking space.

He creped inside the apartment, walked down the hall and into his bedroom, where he found his lover laying in their bed, cuddled up and asleep with another guy. He and his lover had a big fight, for all the drama he had been through and thanked the guy for him confirming the truth.

"He needed a reason to disfigure that motherfucker's ass anyway".

He threw the guys stuff out onto the street, he said, "He sat on the couch laughing about the whole but inside he was really hurting."

Then Tyson asked me all about my last relationship as well.

"Well I'm 26 now, I'm a Cancer, and I was dating this guy from high school Jeffery Holland, you remember him?"

"Well we he was my 1st and only boyfriend, we dated since our teenage years, just like you, everything was good, we even lived together for some time. Then one day, he just changed on me we would argue all the time, it was something every other day.

I came to him with the news about me being accepted into Michigan State and his stuff was gone. He left a letter on the counter saying he was done for sure and he was very sorry about the whole deal that caused us to break up between the two of us, he walked in the door as I was reading the letter and I just looked at him, I wouldn't let him say one word to me.

He tried to explain himself, and I told him, "He could get out of my face and go own about his business and that I'd be very okay."

Not much sooner I had went off to college and that was the last we'd ever see each since we had broking up.

Tyson was looking at me like damn.

"Well I am happy you took some time to come and chill with me Maine."

"Me too you seem like you're a cool guy and I'd like to see you again."

I could feel me getting a bit stuffy so I asked him to crack a window for us a little breeze.

We were having a good time, enjoying each other's company so much and this visit was going so good but it was late and I knew I had to go home. I offered the next time. We would hang at my place.

"I liked that," he said.

I had to go, it was just a short day, but it was a very profound time we shared, and I was looking forward to my next encounter with Tyson.

Chapter 3

Can you believe it's already been 6 months, since I've started working for The Times? I was heading to work on the advice column, where lately I've been getting a few thank you letters from the reader by the way, when this one particular letter swept across my desk.

It read... Dear Mr. Styles,

What should I do? I was dating someone many years ago, we broke up and went our separate ways and then I realized they were the one and I was a jerk, for hurting them badly.

Time has passed and I wanted to meet with them for chance to talk and catch up to resolve our issues and even try to get them back. What should I do?

Signed,

A fan and a reader

I went over to my computer to reply to the letters and addressed this particular writer head on. I gave it this response....

Dear Reader,

1st off you have to take some responsibility for your actions in this. You pray about this and leave it all at the altar of the Almighty. He will set you straight on your path, just believe and have the faith.

Signed,

Mr. Styles

I left work at 4 pm. I didn't have time for lunch that day, so I went to grab a small bite from Mickey D's. Heading home I got a text message from Lena. A guy came thru the area looking for me, he didn't say who he was, and just to tell you "Hi".

My 1st reaction was Tyson, I dialed him up but there was no answer. I made it home right at 4:45P.M. At my apartment, there was an envelope, no name on it, attached to the door. I grabbed it and went inside.

I sat down at the kitchen table, opened the envelope, it was a letter from someone it read...

Dear Jisain,

Surprise! What it do Maine? I haven't heard from you in a long while. I tracked you down here and decided to drop you some lines.

Your sis tells me you finished school, congratulations and that job at the paper, that's all great news, I'm proud of you my man. Tell me something, have you been thinking about me even a small bit, of what we had. Do you think you'll forgive me about the past?

I heard you moved back home, word does travel fast lol. I really have been missing you. The way you cooked those meals, the way we loved on each other.

After you left, I took some time for myself and after two years, six months and so many lonely night and so real long movies without your touch, I knew I needed you back baby.

I don't know if you're in a new relationship or whatever but this has been weighing on my back for so long. I'll see you around boy.

Your old lover and friend,

Jeffery

I tore up the letter and tossed it in the trash. I went down the hall into my bedroom to change cloths. I got a pair jeans and shirt got dressed and found myself in the bathroom sitting on the side of bathtub, crying myself to pieces, I got up from the side of the bathtub, and I looked at myself in the mirror and said,

"It's time for a change Jisain a change."

I cleaned my face up and walked out the door, when my cellphone rang.

"Hello"

"Sup Ji," it was Tyson.

"I was just about to head over to your place now."

"Oh ok, well I'll see you when you get here, but 1st could you stop and get your boy some sweet, chocolate ice cream?"

"Some ice scream, yeah I gotcha," I said as I phone hung it up.

I stopped off at the corner store, to find Tyson's ice cream and I needed to get some gas for the car. I paid for the gas and ice cream and I was out the door. While pumping the gas, a car pulled up on the other side of the pumps, to my surprise it was Jeffery, I was a bit late trying to avoid his presence and it was very obvious once he walked over to me at my car.

My gas was pumping, when he spoke,

> "Hey Jisain, Maine what's the deal?"

> "Really, what can I say Jeffery, you already know the deal with me, so what's up with you and the bitch you dropped me for, up and left you like you did me or you're here to explain yourself again, no need to say a word, I moved on with my life," I got in my car and drove away.

Chapter 4

I made my way to Tyson's without a moment to spare. I got out the car and headed up the stairs to his apartment. I knocked on the door and he came outside and said for me to blindfold myself. I gave him the bag as he handed me the blindfold.

He took my hand, and led me inside the door, I was so nervous because I would have never imagined what was about to happen. I stood there in the doorway, with Tyson there behind me, he took the blindfold off, my eyes opened and there was his mother sitting there smiling ear to ear.

 I at that moment was going through a range of emotions. She got up from the sofa, walked over and gave me a hug. I hugged her back and excused myself to the kitchen.

"Babe, you didn't tell me I was meeting your mother what's up?"

"I love you."

He took my hand and we returned to his mother, waiting for us in the living room. He could feel me trembling as he introduced me to his mother.

"Mama, I want you to meet my bae Jisain."

"Hello Jisain, I'm Ms. Constance, but you may call my, Ms. Coco like my baby Tyson."

I giggled a little.

"Ms. Coco where did that come from?"

"Well I kept it from when she was younger, the family would call her Coco," Tyson answering me from the kitchen.

We sat around and talked and I learned Ms. Coco was the youngest of three children an older brother Joseph and a sister Clara Marie, that she was divorced from Ty's daddy after, 36 years of marriage and she was happy and Tyson didn't have any siblings which was not likely he, acted a little spoiled.

She told me all about the time Tyson came home and told her all about the 1st day he saw me in class.

He said, "Mama when he came in the room, I was stunned by the way he looked in those Maroon and Blue printed jeans and the novelty tee shirt, his hair was taped off, mama he was so hot."

That was so long ago, I still had that shirt, I don't remember those pants, and I think I lost or ruined them in a fight.

We sat down at the table for a little dinner of Fried fish, French fries and garden salad and I asked about Tyson's father.

His father's name was Terrance Lee Jacks the III, after his own father. He had a crazy family, 2 siblings, with a very bad habit of smoking crack cocaine.

Ms. Coco said, "She did love Ty's father but that she had enough of the same crap each and every day. He would work, and then he would come home high. She said she had cooked dinner and they were about to sit down to dinner, when he came in and announced that he had lost the house and that in six months the house was going to be reposed.

I moved out and stayed with Tyson for a little while, I found myself a job got back on my feet and after that I finally divorced him.

He went to rehab then after and he seemed to be getting his life together for a little while, and then he relapsed so bad that he overdosed. We buried him about 2 years ago and life seemed to go on slowly but it went on.

Once we were done with dinner, Ms. Coco and I decided to do the cleaning, where we could talk.

"What was it like when Tyson came out and told you he was gay?"

"It was a year after his after his dad passed away, when Tyson came out to and being honest I kind of knew, because he wasn't dragging any little girls around," Ms. Coco was very blunt, yet very kind.

"Nevertheless I watched him began to feel so much better, and he's as happy as he's ever been in a long time."

After the cleaning, Tyson and I walked his mother out to her car, we hugged and kissed her goodbye around 10, and we headed back up to the apartment, for that long waiting Chocolate ice cream. We sat on the couch watching a movie and I asked him, "What do I do for you?"

He sat back on the couch and he, I guess he was thinking of something to say.

Then he spoke these words.

"When we were in school and you came in the classroom, if you'd seen the look in my eyes, main you were so fucking sexy to look at 1st, I was amazed by you, and now I have you here with me I feel we can do anything we wanted."

He leaned over and kissed me and it was the sweetest, most passionate kiss I'd ever had. Tonight I knew I wanted to take our relationship to the next level. I looked him in his eyes.

"I'm ready Tys."

"You're ready, oh yeah you're ready."

We stood up and started to kiss one another, we slowly pilled the cloths from our bodies, Tyson turned on some Jagged Edge and we sat on the floor. Tyson kissed me all over, he caressed my temples with his hands, I rubbed his body with my fingers and I knew it was on.

He tasted my love and yes it was everything I hoped it would be. He gave my body everything I was craving, I swear he took my breath away and I was so happy we waited as long as we did.

He was so gentle and strong and I was so hot and wet that we just rolled over and over and played inside each other's bodies all night long.

The next morning, I woke up, wrapped inside his arms, in a blanket. Tyson got up and cooked us breakfast. I laid there still sleeping when he called out to me.

"Good morning bae, you good?"

"Yeah baby I am great, what are you doing up so early?"

"I'm cooking breakfast, Maine roll-up."

I got up to get dressed, cleaned up the blanket and pillows from the floor and rolled us a blunt to smoke.

We sat and ate breakfast watching Harry Potter on the TV set.

Today we were both off from work, and I felt like shopping. Tyson gave me something to wear, to my surprise we were both dressed the same. We pulled off at 11:30, in Ty's car, having a discussion about dinner last night.

I told him, "I thought his mother was lovely and I had a great time meeting her."

Over at the mall, we were having a great time, walking around looking at different pairs of Jordan's, when I saw a perfect pair of shoes. They were these baby blue and navy blue Jordan's, that I just fell in love with and had to have them and yes I got them. We went to look at some cloths and we even picked out some pieces for each other.

We were getting hungry so around 2 we decide to go have some dinner at Outback Steak house, we ordered dinner and some drinks.

We got our drinks and we were talking.

"Would you like to go away somewhere for a weekend?"

"Where would we go?"

"Anywhere we want, I just want to go with you. We should celebrate 6 of the most awesome month's bro"

He leaned over the table, kissed my hand and I could feel my knees buckle and my hands got all sweaty.

We got our food and began to enjoy the meal.

"You know what, Texas would be nice, we could go to Six Flags and ride the rides, walk around and eat and have a great time, what do you think about that Tys?"

"Yeah babe, that would be cool, we can take some bud go out there and have us a great damn time."

"So when are we planning to go out?" I asked.

"Well I thought, since your birthday is coming up we could go for that weekend."

We finished our meals, and left for to catch us a movie. We went to see Fools Gold, it was an ok movie, we were sitting there in our seats getting comfortable, and when the movie started he grabbed my hand and kissed it. I knew I didn't feel so afraid of being with him. I leaned over to whisper in his ear I was ready to go.

Tyson drove us to a secret place, he said he came here all the time just to hang out and chill.

He drove up right as the sun was setting on the water, like the water's mirror, it was very beautiful and a nice site to sit and gaze at.

We were sitting there in the car, looking at the waves slowly drifting on and off the bank. Tyson had a cigar and some bud to roll-up. We twisted up a blunt and just relaxed. We took turns blowing each other charges, kissing.

Tyson got a little bit more comfortable and deciding to take off his shirt and leaving on his white-t shirt and opened the sunroof. Tyson placed a c.d. into the system, it was a mixed c.d. he always kept it in the car.

As the track started to play, we let our seats back to stare out at the stars, as they lit up the crisp warm night on June.

We had a conversation, about what happened the 1st time we had sex.

"I was 16 and Jeffery was 17. My aunt and sister were gone to the store and my uncle was out working, and Jeffery would come over like always and hang out with me like any other day, but this day he was acting very strange and different.

We were playing the video game in my bedroom, sitting on my bed, and he just came out and told me that he was crushing on me and I knew my feelings for him, so I followed his lead and told him about my feelings for him.

We began to touch on each other and we kissed and there were sparks all over the place. We stopped kissing, started back playing the game, the tension in the room was growing and we just let nature run its course.

I looked at him, he looked at me and the kissing started once more. We didn't know anything about the whole four play stuff, so I lay there on top of him kissing, I could feel him getting hard and I was steaming.

I got up went to the stash of condoms my Uncle had giving me, (when he thought I was having sex), I gave one to him a condom, I had some lotion on my nightstand and I was on.

I was shacking, I think I was more afraid my Aunt or someone catching us but any event, he was gentle and we made love until we both had an orgasm."

Tyson told me all about his 1st time.

"It was the time he came to visit his family in Cali, he was about 19 when he met a guy that was about 22, and he was sexy.

I built up some courage and walked over to the guy and they begin to talk, he thought Tyson was older by the way he looked.

By the end of the night, he and the guy left the party they were at went to the guy's motel room. In the guy's room, the guy came over, he unzipped my pants and was impressed with my package, he went down on me and he was the bomb too.

I fell on the bed, he gave a rubber, and it was on. The next morning, I woke up with a condom full of nut and I felt like a new man."

He never saw the guy after that, he guessed the guy had taking off.

We were still laying there in the car, looking up at the stars, when a shooting star flew by, right across the sky in our view.

"Make a wish."

"I made this wish so long ago and now it's finally came true, when I met you Tyson," I answered.

I slid over in the seat where Tyson was sitting and he wrapped in arms and we just laid there looking at the stars.

"Where is this headed?" I was getting serious in the moment.

"I don't know babe, but God has us here for a reason, so there no telling," He answered.

"Jisain I want you to know if I never get the chance, I love you."

"I love you too Tyson."

"Can I ask you something?"

"Shoot!"

"What is your view on marriage?"

"I don't know babe, I want to get married one day to the right person."

He was feeling good I would say when he began to climb out the sunroof of the car, when the Tyrese song came on.

"Turn on the lights," He said shouting to me, he was going to dance for me.

I got out the car and sat up on the hood. He was fucking sexy, the way he was beating his chest with his fists, the way he bit his lips, making me laugh, teasing, playing with his cloths, and by the time he got down to his boxers' shorts, I was dripping droll down my fingers.

He slowly walked over to me, he kissed my fingers so gently up to my arms, pulling me down to him, kissing my neck while unbuttoning my pants, letting them slide down to the ground and he turned me downward onto the car, I could feel his body, his nature on my horizon as he kissed me down my back.

I could feel him kissing down my spine and he began to taste my love. I melted the deeper he tasted my juices. When he came up, he turned me to him, picked me up and slid me on the hood of the car.

I was lying there, watching him slip on the rubber. He grabbed my legs, and placed them on his shoulders. He made love to me right then and there. I knew he was the man I had been dreaming he would be.

He was everything I knew I wanted in a man, a friend and a lover. I could feel a small tear fall from my eye, I could feel him about to reach his climax, and I held on tight to him because I was reaching mines at the same time.

He grabbed my hands into his, looking into my eyes saying how much he loves me, I was saying how I much I loved him too.

He was still inside my body stroking harder and deeper. Damn he was going for was going for a second climax. He held my body tightly against his and he blew my mind for the second time and yes I did have another climax.

Chapter 5

This was the craziest day today. I woke up feeling a bit shaky about work, so I took serious caution when into work. In my office letters were piled up to the ceiling. I got to work responding to the letters for the paper and posting some advice to my column, on the website.

As the day progressed, I got a knock at my door. There were 2 florist deliveries for me. The 1st one was White Roses and the other one was arrangement of Lilly's and Orchids, they were both very beautiful. I read the cards that were attached the flowers.

> What's up babe, I just wanted you to know that I love you and I miss, call me later, I love you.

> Tyson

The 2nd one read....

> Hey Jisain, meet me in our place 1 hour today.

> Jeffery

I was shocked, surprised, and confused in that moment. I sat back in my chair in a daze because it was totally unexpected. I was so busy at work that I decided to skip lunch.

I was going home to change and then meet Tyson but 1st I went to meet Jeffery.

He was waiting for me down at the train tracks over the old bridge. As I approached him I told myself to be cool and be calm. I stood there staring at him. He walked over to greet me with a kiss. I tossed my hands up in his face.

> "What? You called me out here for something?"

> "Well Ji, I know I did you wrong but I'm here now to apologize for everything and I'm here to get you back, some way, you were the

only one who really loved me in spite of all the shit I took you through, you loved the man inside and I want that back.

You were there for me, when I lost everything and had no one to love. You remember when my mom's kicked me out the house, you took me in and we were good.

I've loved you forever and I fucked it up, please baby I'm begging you for one more chance, to take me back and be my life, my best friend, my lover again.

Give me back the life I let walked away so long ago, I love you Ji please. We've known each other since we were 8 and 9 years old, we were high school sweethearts."

I watched Jeffery, fall to his knees with tears bleeding from his eyes, squeezing me around my waist.

"Baby you made me whole, in every way possible I need you back."

I turned away from him, looking down at the ground and I took a deep a breath, I turned back to him.

"Look Jeffery man, I can't do it, I thought when we younger, that I would never make a better friend than you, once we hooked up, I thought we were in love.

We were friends for 12 years, neighbors since we were kids and lovers for 4 years, you were my 1st, you taught me so much and yes you gave me the world that you could. I loved you for that but you need to know that I've moved on.

You meant so much to me when we were together, Jeff I used to love you. Those walks to and from school, we would crack jokes. Jr. High we rode the bus to school together, we had some of the same classes, and we even fought together.

You remember high school prom, we didn't have dates so we went to the mall, they kicked us out for making out in the picture booth, (we both laughed at that moment).

I thought you would marry me and that we'd spend the rest of our lives together, and then that day I came home and you left that letter, it broke my heart, the things you said, I knew we were over.

Jeff I've moved on with my life and you should too. I have to go but you keep this in mind, I may have stopped loving you, but it just transcended across the night sky."

He got up from his knees, I turned to walk away from, when he grabs my hand, pulled me toward him and gave me a kiss and for that second my knees buckled down, the way they did when we embraced. I knew it all was wrong for me being there, the kiss, everything.

I got so upset at him, I pushed him, then I turned and ran away, I got in the car, wiping my mouth.

I started my car and drove away. In the car I called my sister, I told her what happened, and she was in shocked and very upset not only with Jeffery but with me too for my part.

When I got to her house, I just broke down in a mad rage of tears, that I just fainted. When I woke up I was in Tyson's arms wrapped up me in him.

"Baby is you okay?"

"No I'm not baby my ex kissed tonight, I'm sorry but he just grabbed me and he kissed me"

"Where is this nigga at, I want to talk to him, Ji why did you even meet this buddy ass dude, anyway?"

"Babe I went to him, I told him that we me and you were dating, and that he and I was not getting back together, I walked away, he grabbed me and he kissed me, where you going?" he was walking away from me.

"I'm going to find this cat and talk to him for a minute?"

"Well I'm going with you, I trust you but right now your upset and I don't want you to do anything crazy Tyson."

I called Jeffery and asked him if he'd meet us at the Moon bar on the balcony.

"Alright baby I just want to talk to him and tell 'em to get his fucking mind right."

When we got to the Moon bar, Tyson paid the doorman and we headed up the stairs, out to the balcony. Jeffery was sitting at a table, with about 4 drinks with a 5th one in his hand, totally intoxicated.

We sat down on the opposite side of the table. He sat up and saw us in his full view.

"What's up Ji, Maine what's up, you guys wanted to meet with me?"

"I want you to meet someone, this is my lover Tyson," I said in a shaky voice.

"Damn baby stop trembling, Look Jeffery I know the deal between you and Jisain, and I tried to let it pass, because I love him, but that kissing shit really pissed me off.

I'm here to tell you to move on, I'm the man that's with him, I love everything about him and you fucked up and lost him.

I just want to let you know that this is it, this is the last time we'll have this discussion."

We stood up from the table and headed for the door, when Tyson went flying into a wall, it was Jeffery he was attacking him, within seconds Tyson had turned around, giving Jeffery the blues, with a single punch to the jaw, as Jeffery fell through the crowd, I grabbed Tyson's hand and we ran out the club to his car.

We were chilling out driving to my apartment, Tyson reached into his glove box and lite up a blunt.

We made it to my apartment safely, once we were inside Tys and I headed for the shower, he held me in his arms, and he whispered in my ear.

"Baby I'd never hurt you the way that dude did you, baby look at me, with the tears in his face, do you love me, do you really want this shit to work, because I do Ji.

You're making my heart feel something I never thought was possible, you make me want to buy the whole mall for you, shower you with the things you know you deserve. Serve your meals on gold platters, but that's something I can't do.

All I can do is love you Jisain, open the door for you, hold your hand when were out enjoying our time together, and give you all of me with no hesitation. Baby every day that I've been with you I been falling more and more in love with you, that smell of Vanilla Sugar on your skin, how soft your body felt against mine when we 1st made love, how you just be yourself when I come around, I just want us to make this something to share."

He dropped to his knees.

"Jisain baby tell me something, do you want me?"

I sat on my knees facing him.

"Tyson I made a mistake and I'm wrong but he's not you and will never be I love you."

We finally got out of the shower, dried off and sat down on the couch. I was feeling very tense, so Tyson decided to give me a back rub. I lay across his lap and he went to working out the tension in my back with his hands of magic.

I was beginning to relax when I could feel his soft lips kiss my legs, down to my thighs. He slowly lowered his body onto mine. I could feel his nature on my surface, he reached into the drawer for a condom, slipped it on, and it was all greenlights from there.

He stroked deeper and deeper while messaging my spine, kissing my neck, and we were making love with his head on mine. He pulled me up to him, I could feel the heat rising between us, and the sweat from our bodies became pure oils as he went harder.

I could hear him saying the lyrics to my favorite love song "Sweet Lady" in my ear, the more he said those lyrics, he held me tight in his arms, I could feel my climax about to peak, and Tyson was reaching his climax. Moments later we both had a big finish, he held my hands squeezing them in his.

We fell to sleep wrapped in each other arms, where I know I wanted to be. Here with him holding me close to his body, in his heart and on his mind.

Chapter 6

The next morning, I woke up and I was extremely late for work. I reached for my phone and I called to work. I told them I was unavailable to come in for work, it was cool because the column had already been done and I had some family business I had to get done only today.

After the call, I could feel Tyson kissing my neck.

"I'm the family business your tending to I guess huh?"

"Yeah, you are Bae!!"

I got up from the couch, heading into my bedroom to find some cloths to throw on.

"What were your plans today," Tyson was calling out to me from the other room.

"Well I was planning a trip by the clinic for a checkup, what about you?"

"Well I'm off today, I offered to do something with my moms, but 1st I'll come with you, I haven't been tested in the last few months anyway"

We headed to the Health Unit which wasn't too far from my place.

At the clinic we gave them our information and had a seat to wait for our number to be called. They called us in and I was nervous because it was my 1st time being there with my lover, while they asked you those personal questions. Before I knew it we were saying those words "Were partners" Tyson grabbed my hand and kissed it. They looked at me then Tyson.

"Well the last time you were here Mr. Styles you were younger, now here's a guy who's not too shy to be here with you," asked the doctor.

"Well can we get this over please?" I was getting impatient.

20 minutes later the testing was done and we were waiting for our results. The nurse called us back and gave us the news that all was well health wise and that we were healthy and to remember to practice safe sex.

Tyson asked could he borrow my car.

I didn't mind. He dropped me off at my apartment then Tyson went to meet with his mother, they went to have dinner and talk.

"Ma talk to me, tell me what I should do, it's been 6 months, since Jai and I been dating. Jisain and I are talking about taking a trip for his birthday.

What you think I should get my babe. I know he's into music, food and shoes."

"Well baby take mama's advice and go with your heart, whatever you feel, take it and put it in motion. Let me tell you what your father did that won me over.

He knew all the little things meant so much to me. He took me to dinner at my favorite place Tis Amore', he had a violinist playing near the table that evening and when the place was about to close, he had the owner come over to the table and had him read a poem that he had written for me when we were in high school.

We had been dating 6 years that night he proposed it was magical," tears fell from her eyes as she told the story.

"Me I know what I'm going to do."

Tyson dropped off Mrs. Coco, but little did I know he had something cooking up his sleeve for me.

Chapter 7

Well today seemed to be more normal than ever. I went to work, there didn't seem to anything going on, no letter for the advice column, so I went online and just giving my readers some insight to who I was really and letting the readers know I'm a real person just like them who didn't always the answers to all their problems.

I got a call from Tyson he wanted me to pick him up from work that evening, and that became my plans for after I got off work.

It was 5:00 when I left work, to go pick up Tyson from work. I pulled up to a large building where it looked like they did construction. Tyson came out the front entrance dressed in his white wife beater, black jeans covered in paint he wore his company hard hat and looked so good that I wanted to bite him on the chest.

As he got inside the car he kissed my cheek.

> "What's up, baby you okay?"

> "Yeah I'm good, just ready for this trip."

We drove off down the road and he began asking me a lot of questions that dealt with my interests, I answered the questions, when we were driving past a Freemans Jewelry Shop.

> "Pull in, let's go look at something for mom's birthday is coming up and I wanted to look at something's for her."

We walked inside the shop to look at some pieces they had to offer, we tried on some pieces, and he saw a beautiful watch that caught his attention, he was stuck looking it.

The gold was magnificent, it was crafted in a sapphire shape, and I could tell he loved it. It was priced at $950 dollars.

We walked over to the necklace counter, where I caught a glimpse at a gold rope, my eyes where the size of a quarter, I couldn't take my eyes away from the shiny piece of bling, it beamed like light shining inside a window seal in awe, I knew I had to have it when, Tyson came over and saw the look on my face.

"Baby do you want it," he asked, at 1st I didn't answer.

He asked again, "Ji do you want it baby?"

I jumped the moment he grabbed my hand, "Yeah, yes baby I love it."

Tyson asked the clerk for the price of the gold rope it was $350 dollars.

"Ty what are you doing?" I was getting excited.

He took some money from his pocket, counted out the dollar amount and gave it over to the clerk. The clerk gave him the receipt and wrapped the necklace.

We walked out the door to the car, got into the car, and Tyson turned to me.

"I wanted this to happen at Six Flags but seeing the look in your eyes, happy birthday baby", as he placed the gold rope around my neck.

In the car we were discussing our plans for the evening and we agreed to hit a gay club afterwards we have some breakfast at IHOP, and then we'd both head home for work the next day.

The time was 6:00pm when I finally arrived home from dropping off Tyson to get himself together for our date while I did the same.

As I made my way to the apartment, I couldn't help but notice my neighbor sitting in the stairway, he was smoking some herb, so I made conversation.

"Maine that shit smells good, sup I'm Ji, Jisain"

"Sup I'm Cameron Carter, but everybody calls Carter."

"You smoke Main you can hit this if you want to."

I sat down beside him on the stairway and puffed on the herb a few times and it was a hit.

"I'm planning a date with my boyfriend. You and your friend should come if y'all want."

"Oh yeah Kool, what time you leaving out?"

"Around 11:30 at the latest once he gets over here, I'll come downstairs and get you when you leave out."

I got inside and got my cloths out for the club and got things together for the evening. I laid down for a nap. When I got up it was 11:15, Tyson was knocking at my door.

He came in the door for me smiling so gently. I got dressed and we were out the door. I stopped at Carter's apartment for him and his boyfriend and lite up some more herbs that went into an instant rotation.

When we arrived at the club Tyson and I were both in a great mood. We danced and laughed, I could tell he was into me by the way he held me close on the dance floor, and we were in tune with each other and we were having a great time.

Later that evening the club had their show with the entertainers, we grabbed us a table and sat watching the show. I was looking at Tyson's face as the show went on and it got me to thinking that maybe I could do something like that, I had a great body and I knew how to move my body, so that would make for good conversation at breakfast.

I had worked up a thrust, I asked Tyson to get me a drink from the bar, we went to sit out on the back patio to finish my drink and smoked some more herb before the party started back up. After our break out on the deck, we headed back into the club down to the dance floor and got back to having a great time.

The club had a great deejay host her name was Alicia she was a cool chick, with a nice figure, was dressed really cute, she had a great personality and she slamming on the mic, the way she had the crowd intoxicated with her joy she fumed into the room.

It was the last call we were on our way out the door to the breakfast when she called out to Carter. Carter went over to talk to Alicia after about 10 minutes she and husband also were headed to have breakfast with us over at IHOP.

At IHOP we sat around the table the couples sat face to face to each other. Everyone went around the table and introduced ourselves.

> "Carter, me, Scooter Alicia's husband, Lee was Carter's boyfriend and Tyson."

The conversation seemed to shine that evening, we all ordered breakfast and we were waiting for the food to come to the table.

"So what's the deal with the club," Lee asked?

"Well we can't seem to keep the spot open," said Alicia.

"Well it a great place for us to hang and kick it," I said.

"I think I'll go every week," said Tyson.

"Well I'm down for that," said Carter.

Our food finally came, there were Colorado omelets and pancake everywhere you looked, and the conversation was cut short with everyone cleaning our plates, we looked like men fresh from jail enjoying his first meal in new freedom in years. After breakfast we paid our bills and went our separate ways.

We made it home just before 3 am. We bid our farewells and Tyson and I retired to my apartment for the bedroom, I hit the pillows and down for the count I was, Tyson had wrapped me up in his arms under the sheets.

"I love you baby." his words covered my heart but I was asleep.

Chapter 8

With the trip just weeks away Tyson and I decided to dive into work and to give each other some space just to chill and get some money saved.

I stayed busy with the advice column, having a great yet challenging time giving some much needed advice to people across the city. After work I was only interested in was a hot shower to drain the pain from my tired body. I got dressed in little to nothing and I was feeling great.

I went to the kitchen and looked around for something I could easily prepare for dinner. Chicken nuggets and mashed potatoes were on the menu to cook and sat down on the sofa, got my box of herb and rolled me up a treat. My phone started to buzz it was a text message from Tyson.

He asked me about my day.

I replied it was over and that I was cooking some dinner.

He replied he was doing the same and that he missed me.

I texted him back saying to come by and hang out with me and play the game or something.

I had my meal and I decided to lie down for a nap.

I was awakened by a knock at the door and I knew it was Tyson. I got up in a daze and answered the door and let him in. I got back in my place on the sofa and he joined me in his sweat shorts just as I was.

"Did you have a good day at work?"

"Yeah I had a great day baby, I was only thinking mostly of you," he replied, as he squeezed me tightly in him arms.

"That's what's up yo. You know you're really under my skin you know that right."

"Well as long as we're being honest, let me ask you something, why do you love me like you do?"

I turned over to him and laid my head upon his chest and I told him.

"I am uplifted every time you come around. It makes my day a little bit brighter, my spirits full of joy when I speak to you on the phone and really back in the days at school I kept an eye on you."

"You did well tell me something I was involved in this?"

"Well freshman year, you were on the basketball team, you got in the poetry club and you were really good. I remember the poem you wrote for English class all the girls and the teacher we're all crying and secretly I thought you wrote it about me.

Jr I meant sophomore year you got on the football team and made the team number 15 that was you, I didn't know you could rap until you entered the talent show. Your song "One God" was really impressive.

Jr year you got in R.O.T.C. we were in the same class, company, and platoon. I was the platoon leader and you'd acted like you knew the drills when I knew you really didn't, and there was football again, where you made Homecoming court and made Jr. Prince and you got voted most likely to succeed by the class.

And senior year we had computer lit class together as well as English IV you sat behind me, you were prom king which was funny because you didn't play any sports, but you did stay in R.O.T.C. and became 1st squad leader, I even remember the poem you wrote when you talked about losing your friend Jimmy Bean in the shooting at the Jamboree game, you missed like a week of school."

"Okay you did your homework, Maine your good really good."

"Oh yes I do get my man and you are my man aren't you."

"I am your man, the one only for you."

He kissed me on the cheek and we fell asleep.

When I woke the next morning, on the breakfast table was breakfast and Tyson had written me a nice note. I had breakfast, got dressed and headed out the door to work.

In the car, my phone begins to buzz, it had several missed event, and I waited until I got to work to finally check my events.

I opened my phone to the six events, two voicemails, one text message, one picture mail and missed call. The text was from Tyson asking me about breakfast this morning, and the note. I replied to the message that I loved it.

The photo was a selfie of Tyson he was smiling so softly. The missed call was my sister, and the two voicemails were my sister and Jeffery.

The message was from Jeffery, saying he was in jail since the fight the other night at the Moon Bar and wanted me to come visit him in jail.

I hung up my cell phone and got to work, there was a pile of letters, so one by one, until around lunch time, I was so hungry I was eating chewing gum, when I got a knock at the door it was Tyson with lunch, he came in, closed the door, and had a seat right on my desk. He sat down with some taco salads from On the Border.

I was thinking we could go to a movie, Will Smith's new movie I AM LEGEND was coming out soon.

We finished lunch and he kissed me on the way out, and said he'd text me later than evening.

I got back to work and 30 minutes later I got a phone call from an unknown number, I answered it.

"Yes this is Jisain."

"Oh hey, Ji its Jeffery"

"I just got home decided to hit you up."

"When you get out?"

"Last night I just came from a job interview, today didn't get 1 yet, but I'm looking for a job."

"I'm happy to hear you doing ok, what made you call me anyway, I should have a restraining order on your ass since the last time I ran into you."

"Well I had to call you and say sorry about all that shit that went down I know I was wrong about everything but you know how I feel about you."

"I want you to meet someone."

"Well were going to the movies tonight I convinced them to come to meet us for dinner."

"Ok I'll call you."

The newspaper was nearly ready for my column, so I quickly finished my page and got it down to the editors before print and I was off to the Regal to get the movie tickets for tonight. I went home and grabbed some cloths for the movie and drove down to my sister's place.

She said she had some news about Jeffery's new lover, Lucy told me she was a woman.

I instantly started to laughing, she said, "her name was Khadijah, did you check you freaking messages."

"Girl I really need a new outfit, get that baby ready, were going shopping."

I was outdone with this news.

In the car, we were cruising, listening to some 90's hip-hop music.

When Tyson called me again, I answered.

"Hey baby! What's up we're headed to the mall you want to meet us here."

He was headed home, he told me to pull over, and I pulled over.

He said, "His mom died last night," he started crying, she died peacefully in her sleep, she had a brain hemorrhage and died.

"Baby I coming right to you, where are you?"

I drove over to his place. I called his name. He was sitting in the bedroom at the edge of the bed with Miss. Coco. Picture in his arms in a long daze I stood in the doorway, looking at him.

I knew what Tyson was feeling in that very moment. He looked at me his face was still traced in his tears, and covered with pain.

"Baby I am so so sorry."

I slowly walked over to him, I sat beside him, I laid my head on his shoulder, and his head fell over on mine.

Tyson cried out, "Why moms God, she was the only person I had left, she made me into the man that I am, "He was shouting.

"She made the man I love so much. I know she wouldn't want you here soaking your life away baby. You know you have her love in your heart."

He sat up looking at me, "You'll get through this, and you know you have me here with you." I said encouraging him.

They gave me two weeks paid time off, so that's good for now baby, can you get me the phone I have to make some calls and get things prepared, I'll be okay, you said you're going be here with me through this," He was trying to cheer up.

"You hungry, I'll get us some food."

"Yeah Chinese baby, I'd like that."

I grabbed my keys and I headed out the door, I called Carter and told him what was happened, I told him to come over to the house.

I got the food, when I returned back to Tyson's place, he was freshly dressed, and I saw him cleaning things that didn't need to be clean.

"I see you're on your feet, would you like some orange glazed chicken, shrimp fried rice?" I was trying to bright him up and I did, he was smiling.

"That's it smiles I can count it all joy, you'll be okay."

We sat around eating and talking. Tyson asked me to go with him over to his mom's to clean in the morning.

"Yes sure I'll go with you I'm with you until the end of this."

I kissed his cheek, for a while we lay around on the couch, and watched movies. Tyson fell asleep in my arms, I got up from the couch, to go take a shower, in the shower I found myself thinking about my mom and dad, I starter to pray....

God I come to you right now in the mist for my lover and my friend Tyson, I'm trusting you to take care of him like you took care of me and my sister.

I'm praying to you in his time struggle and I'm praying to you to heal his heart and that he gets stronger and that he will get over this hill in his life, in Jesus name.

Amen

Chapter 9

We woke up around noon, got dressed in basketball shirts and shorts and were out the door, to head over to Mrs. Coco's house for the cleaning.

When we pulled up, I saw this house it was beautiful, it was fenced in. You would see this house on the upscale side of town, with the neatly cut grass and flowers planted around the pathway to the garage.

We walked inside the door, entering this huge living room that was well decorated. We headed down this hall covered in family photographs, to her bedroom. Her room colors were Cream and Lavender, and she had the softest bed you ever feel. Her cloths were very glamorous cloths, gowns, dresses, and shoes wall to wall. Her bathroom was very lovely, with a nice gold finished tub. This house was everything a home should be.

I stopped Tyson in the bathroom.

"Baby you should stay here in your mom's house, I am sure she would want you to want you here, and I am sure she took care of things here."

"Only if you move in with me?"

I laughed at 1st but the look in his face said he was serious.

"Oh your serious, I can't."

"I know it's only been a few months since we started dating, I did want to move in here but not like this and not so soon 1st, what do you think?"

"I'll think about it and give it some time to sink in."

"Ok you think about it then, take all the time you need."

We left his mother's bedroom and walked down the hall to Tyson's bedroom, before he opened the door his said.

"I was the 1st person to see his bedroom so it's right that I was here."

He took my hand, when he opened the door, I fell in love with his king-sized bed with a cherry wood frame, he had 2 walk in closets and it was very well constructed, the room was colored in Chrisom and black with a lazy boy and flat screen TV set.

"Damn babe Mama Coco did a great job with your room, I love her style", I was impressed with all the class.

I'm happy moms designed my room, she just asked me what I wanted and she did the rest, I always had a room at home, just didn't think I'd come back like this," and he fell on the floor, tears flowing down his face, I held him as he cried.

I cleaned his face and we returned to his mom's room. We went to pack some of her 100's of cloths to give to Goodwill, when he came he came across a letter, it was in an envelope that sat on her dresser. He took the letter, called me into the family room where he proceeded to read the letter.

Dear Tyson,

I knew one day I had to come out and tell you this secret but I couldn't tell you, there was never a right time and then your father died. When you were a little boy, you remember you were 6 or 7 years old.

Your father and I were having some problems, we separated and I met a guy during that separation and I had an affair, your father knew all about it.

I had a sent you to stay at mothers for a little while, during that time, I conceived a child, a son, your brother, he's been living with his father.

His father's name is Kinsten Charles Rumble he lives here in Shreveport, your brother's name Rico Leon Rumble.

He's getting older and I think it's time for you 2 to finally meet. I've placed an address on the back of a picture in the envelope.

Baby I raised you to be a strong black man and I hope you found someone to make and keep you whole as you did in Jisian, I love you and your brother as much as I loved your father.

I also have a message for Jisain love only finds you once in a lifetime.

I think he did right to find you because I see how you've changed my son with your love. I love you both dearly.

Dearest Mother,

Mrs. Coco

I was balling away when he finally finished the letter and looked at me.

"Baby you know she's right Ji, I love you don't cry, "He was wiping the tears away from eyes."

"I'm not going anywhere, you better believe that."

Tyson called up the team and I called my sister, to come over to the house and share the news.

When everyone got to the house we were all sitting around in the lounging room, having some drinks.

"Well I am moving in this is my house and I found out that I have a brother."

We sat around and talked for a while, it was around 11 'o'clock when everyone decided to retire and leave for the evening.

For the next few days, I watched Tyson walk back and forth, looking at the letter the same way, again and again, I grabbed his hand and sat him on the sofa.

"It's time to call your brother and his father, they should know what happened with your mother, and he should get this information from you."

"I always wanted a little sibling growing up and I got one."

"Okay I'll do this for moms, you are right she'd want things to be right, I'll call them."

I handed Tyson the phone. He dialed the number. The phone rang before someone answered the line.

> "Hello, uh this is weird, but name is Tyson, my mother's Mrs. Coco Jacks, passed away 2 days ago, I found a letter she wrote to me about you and your son Rico, and I am requesting that you and Rico come to her service Sunday at Peaceful Rest Church, I'll be in touch with you guys.

> Tell Rico, I can't wait to meet him thank you and good bye." He hung up the phone.

It was Friday the day of Mrs. Coco's wake and all the family of Tyson's family were all arriving over the course of the day, Tyson's family was coming over to the house to visit with Tyson and get to the bottom of things with Rico and Kinsten.

The house was spotless, when his family begins to arrive.

Tyson called me into the family room.

> "Jisain I want you to meet my Uncle Joseph, Aunt Patricia his wife, and my cousin Jalisa, my aunt Clara, uncle Pete her husband and my other cousin LaTonya.

> I want you all to meet my lover and good of friend mines and moms this is Jisain this is his family, his sister Lucy, her husband LaDorian and their baby girl Mariah."

> "I see we all have something in common, we all have daughters," said Mrs. Clara.

Our friends came by the house to show their support, for the wake as well. All the ladies were in the kitchen doing the cooking, while we sat around discussing Mrs. Coco, Tyson asked about Rico.

"Uncle Joe, tell me the truth is this boy my brother," He asked.

"He's your brother no doubt, remember when you came to California that year and stayed with your grandmother, that's was when it all happened, your mother had straightened things out but Rico was a part of her life just as ours."

We ate dinner, a short time after we were off to the church, the services were wonderful and everyone spoke so highly of mother Coco.

After the wake, Tyson and I headed home, he wanted to talk for a while.

"Baby all this talk about my mom's and Rico has me really bugging out," Tyson was all shaken up.

"Well let's smoke and I'll just keep you company," taking my herb stash from my pocket, and I rolled up several smokes for us.

We smoked and sat there for a while I told Tyson we should pray about this that God gives you strength that God was going to fix it all.

We got down on our knees and Tyson prayed....

"Dear Lord,

Since I was a young man, I've always known you to be real in my life, constantly making a way out of no way.

I know I speak with you every day but now in this time Lord, I think I need you more than ever. I'm asking for you to pull me and my family through this hard time.

I pray this guy and his son embrace me and except me the way you, my family, and friends as well. I love you God, for it all, thank you for my bae Jisain and you Lord keep pouring out my blessings.

In Jesus name we,

Amen"

"That was an awesome prayer, you are amazing, when all this is over, and I got a treat for you when we take our trip."

This morning we had to prepare for the services, we had some breakfast and a short time after we got dressed and headed out to meet the rest of the family at the church, where Mother Coco had a lot of people there to pay their condolences.

Tyson parked the car, he had said a quick silent prayer for strength and peace, and we headed to the limousine, Tyson was asking me not to leave his side and I assure him I wasn't, He was still feeling a bit down, I could tell.

At the church, the services were remarkable and powerful. Clare and Joe had a moment to speak of their sister, which was very touching.

In the middle of the service, Kinsten and Rico came walking down the aisle to view Mother Coco's body that final time, Rico couldn't hold himself together when he finally fell apart. Tyson ran over to him, he picked his brother up from the floor and he hugged him as Rico cried.

After the service, we headed to the burial ceremony, thereafter Tyson, Rico, Kinsten and the rest of us headed back to the family house. We sat around talking and eating just having good family fun.

Tyson and Rico had talked and decided that Rico would stay over with Tyson that night, and that we would bring him back home the next day if it was okay with Kinsten. Tyson was excited to have a brother to beat up and hang out with like I did with Lucy.

Later that evening the family had all retired for the night, I found Tyson lying across Mrs. Coco's bed.

"Now you should feel somewhat better huh?"

"Yeah baby I'm happy, you know Rico looks like me and moms, that defiantly my lil brother," he was smiling so huge.

It was the last week for Tyson being off work. When I got up, Tyson and Rico were up already cooking breakfast and they seem to be having a good time, we all sat down at the table said grace and had our breakfast.

Tyson asked Rico, "What did he know about girls?"

"Enough."

"So you are smart enough to know what's going on here with Jisain and me huh?"

"Yeah, y'all are what they call Partners."

"So you are okay with gay people, that you really don't have a problem with it all?"

"You are my big brother. I can't do anything but respect and accept you."

"Alright enough, what are you two getting into," I was changing subject.

"Well it's a surprise," Tyson winked at me.

"Well I have a surprise for you later on, after you and the kid is done having fun right, I've got to get to work, I love you Tys, call me later."

On my way to work, I got a call from Jeffery. I guess he was upset with me.

"Where have you been hiding, I've been trying to catch up with you," he asked.

"I've been with Tyson his mother died last week, don't you read the paper?"

"I wanted to ask you if we could get together, I'd like for you to meet Khadijah."

"How is she, yes I've heard all about her," me in the middle of his confession.

"I've been trying to explain things to you lately, she and I have been having some problems and I found out she's pregnant, I don't know what to do."

"Well talk to her, and ask her what's the deal, let her know all that's wrong and work it out. You want someone without all the work, take your time and talk and work it out that's what I would do," I hung up the phone.

When I got to work, my coworkers and my supervisor were all gathered around and he told them, to get back to work. He knew all about Mrs. Coco she was a contributor to him get his small business open. He told me I could take some time off being a member of the family.

I headed back to Tyson's to share the news with him and Rico, when I had arrived back at the house, they had cleaned the house and were sitting around playing the video game, and Tyson had some herb burning.

I spoke to them, I could see he was already beginning to move his things into the house, and Tyson said he was going to sell the rest of his things for some extra money.

I was lying across the bed when he and Rico came into the room.

"Let's go today, let's just pack some cloths and head down to Texas," he said.

"I'll get my girlfriend on the phone," Rico was shouting as he ran down the hall.

"We got a trip awaiting us and were wasting time," he said.

By noon we had packed some cloths and were on our way to pick up Rico's girlfriend, Brittney before we headed off down the highway for Texas.

Chapter 10

We had been driving for hours, while Tyson played the copilot and the film director, with the instructions and camcorder. We were having a great time seeing the country side, stopping for bathroom breaks and taking pictures in some interesting yet beautiful sites along the route to Texas.

It was 4:30 when we finally drove into Dallas, when we saw a breath taking view of lights up from the freeway.

We talked and got to know each other Lil' Rico and Brittney had been dating for 3 years and they seemed to be serious. Tyson wanted to know we're they having sex asking, them about their sex life.

They said, "They wanted to get married 1st before they went that far with their relationship."

They sound to be level headed enough to be trusted, which was good enough for both of us.

We finally arrived in Arlington, you could see Six Flags from of the freeway, and the excitement filled the car in moments of our arrival. We were another 10 miles from the hotel.

We arrived at the Radisson hotel, we went inside the lobby to the counter, asked for 2 rooms, and paid for them. They showed us to our rooms before we could unpack the car. We were on the 3rd floor across the hall from one another.

We headed back to the car grabbed our bags and took the up to our rooms. Tyson and I decided to get us some dinner. We made sure Rico and Brittney were okay before we left out to find something good for dinner.

We found a nice Chinese place around the corner, ordered some food and headed back to the hotel. Tyson had delivered Rico and Brittney their dinner over to their room and came to join me.

We had a nice balcony we could sit out on and have dinner and take in the view around the city.

I had packed some herb for us to enjoy, Tyson was kind enough to roll us several treats to smoke before we ate dinner. We sat out on the balcony smoking, taking in the sites of the city, letting the herb smoke blow in the wind.

That night played the Isley Brothers while we sat around in the Jacuzzi tub with the bubbles dancing around our stiff bodies from such a long drive. I sat in Tyson's lap as he rubbed my back with the Hot Cocoa oil, when his hands caught a grasp to my body, and I became as soft as cotton.

While he was rubbing me down I could feel my toes curl, I bit my lip, Tyson's touch had overwhelmed me, I could feel his kisses on my neck and it was on. We began to kiss, we had some foreplay fun. That night was so much more than any other night we've ever shared.

Tyson said, "I wanted to do something different tonight."

"Okay he was willing to try something different tonight."

I guess he had some new tricks up his sleeve because he worked my body out, and I had my chance to make love to Tyson and I wasn't going to let it pass.

I was ever so gentle to his body with every stroke I could hear him groan and moan as his hands took hold to my own. The climax was one of the most powerful moments we've have ever had.

That night we laid in bed, I asked him, "How was he feeling?"

"I'm okay just now that the hard part was over, and that his mother was resting."

He was holding me tight and he was quite for a moment.

He said, "I had a dream about moms last night, Rico and I were at her gravesite, she was standing there looking over us, standing there together.

She was happy to see her kids to be together, that she loved us and she was with my dad, before I woke up she gave me a message for you, "In the short time of getting to know Jisain, she knew you were good for me and that she loved you."

When Tyson woke up this morning he went to Rico to tell him about the dream, he started to cry and Tyson said,

"I am here now and I'm going through this with you brother."

We slept the night away around 2 a.m. I rolled over I couldn't feel Tyson's arms nor his body in bed, I sat up looking around for him, and he was sitting at the edge of the bed watching the TV, but there was a blank look on his face.

"Tyson what's wrong, are you okay?"

I smelled the herb burning in the air. I sensed he was letting off some steam.

"Yeah I'm cool baby, just thinking about my folks and everything in my life, to see if it all makes sense any more than it did back then," he said.

"What is it to think about, come back to bed, and I'll hold you, Tyson you have to get some rest baby you know that right?"

He crawled back up to me, laid his head upon my chest as I began to rock us slowly back to sleep, I was told him.

"Tomorrow will be a new day, and that things are going to get better."

Then next morning, when I woke up Tyson was coming back with breakfast, I crawled out of bed, greeted him with a hug and kiss.

"Good morning babe."

"Good morning Papo."

We sat in bed, watching cartoons like children, having breakfast.

"How are Rico and Brittney?"

"They're good Rico went downstairs to get breakfast with me."

After we had breakfast we cleaned the room, had showered, got dressed and headed downstairs.

We took some pictures before we got in the car and made our way over to Six Flags. In the car there were a bunch of laughter and joy in the air.

Six Flags was perfect. Tyson and I walked hand in hand. He talked me onto some of the rides. Magic Mountain was crazy with the darkness, twists, the loops and turns but we were having a great time, we had a blast. The Mr. Freeze ride it was insane, and we loved the Batman ride.

I didn't know Rico and Tyson were such good basketball players, scoring prizes for both me and Brittney. We found a wood craving shop that craved our nicknames into our favorite colors.

Tyson found some of his cartoon character items in the Looney Toons shop, he loved him some Daffy Duck as much as I loved some Taz, we took thousands of pictures, we ate like horses and had a great at time the park until they closed at 10:30, we headed for the exit back to the car.

We decided to go and see a movie. Meet the Browns was showing that night. The night was perfect, after the movie, we headed in for the night.

In the room, Tyson and I decided to have some fun. I had surprised him with a pair of silk boxers. They were blue covered with playboy bunnies on them. Tyson gave me a show. He loved it when I threw dollar bills at him at him for my private show.

I also showed off some of my moves, twisting and bending my body slowly removing my shirt and shorts from my then chilled skin, we embraced, he carried me over to the bed and that night Tyson was in full overload.

After the passion we laid there in bed, I could tell Tyson was getting over this hill in his life, I think we were feeling very lucky.

Chapter 11

After a long 2 weeks, I was very feeling refreshed. I had finally made the decision to stay in my place, I couldn't break my lease so early in to move in with Tyson.

I called him and told him my decision and he seemed to be okay with it, because our relationship was so fresh we didn't want to miss with a good thing by moving in together so early.

I was in the apartment, when Carter came by.

"What's up Maine, how you been doing"

"Well I'm good, we just got back from out of town and that Tyson's finally get settled in over at the house."

"I need some advice. My bae and I are some having some problems, I keep doing shit to hurt him, I love him, he loves me, there's nothing we want do for one another, what should I do?"

"Well you and him should get in church, pray together and grow in God. He's brought Tyson and me closer than ever, so my advice to you is to just pray that we grow stronger in the Lord."

"You know Ji, that make sense, I'll try that Maine, well I'm getting out of here got to go meet bae, he's getting off work, I'll get back with you later, just call me homie."

I was headed to work, in the car listening to the radio talking about the election being days away and that we should know the issues and get out there and vote.

Work was very smooth. I got the column finished, for the printer.

I left for the day and headed over to meet Tys. At the house, he was in the out in the driveway, grabbing the last of his things from his apartment. I was getting out of the car when he came and greeted me with a hug and a kiss.

"What's up babe?"

"I'm good now Papo, seeing your sexy self."

I grabbed a box from his car, helping him take his things into the house, walking down the hall to his bedroom, where he had begun to change things around.

"I saw you changed the room around and you even made closet space, you really wanted me to move in here." He had also moved his bed over to the wall with the Lazy boy to its left side.

I could really tell he was serious about us moving in together.

"Babe what's up, it time to clean this closet and get rid of some of these old cloths".

We began unpacking his boxes of clothes to hang in the closet, when we were done, we went through some of his old clothes and there was so much stuff.

"You should give these clothes to Rico, I'm sure your brother would like that once you clean them up and everything."

"That's what I am doing now bae, I've been washing all morning," Tyson said with his warm smile.

"Oh ok Forgive Me Sire'."

He led me down the hall to the wash room to let me see his progress, there were basket of clothes needed to be folded, so we grabbed the baskets of clothes and headed over to the living room to the couch and turned on the t.v. for the presidential debate was on so we tuned in.

Barack Obama was doing very well especially calling out his opponent John McCain out on the issues we needed to be aware of as a country and things we were not as well, so we were happy we caught that. With only two loads left I took a break to cook dinner.

While I cooked, he called out to me.

"Baby"

"Yeah Bae"

"How do you feel about taking picture for the house?"

"That's cool with me, when do you want to have them done?"

"I'll let you know when, you just be ready."

"Okay you got a deal then Tys."

Tonight was special, our 1st meal in the new house, we sat at the table Tyson and I said grace.

"Dear Lord,

We come to you giving you thanks for our 1st meal in this new house, my new home. Ji and I thank you for the many blessings you have giving us and the life you have blessed us with so much, I love him Lord and I thank you for each and every day, these thing and all things we ask in your strong and powerful Lord

Amen"

Dinner was a simple cornbread casserole dish and we drunk Cherry Lemonade.

After dinner I did the dishes, Tyson went to start the last basket of laundry then he headed to the shower to the shower, I could hear the water running, Tyson came and grabbed my hands, dragging from the kitchen, into the bathroom.

"What are you doing babe?" I said screaming in laughter.

He was laughing painfully hard, when he pulled me into the shower getting my clothes wet, he began to kiss me passionately, my top lip, then biting my bottom lip, (which he knew drove me crazy).

Tyson undressed me, my shirt then my pants which by this time were drenched in water, then I undressed him throwing his wet clothes on the floor, we embraced once more.

Once we were naked, I sat down with Tyson in between my legs. I bathed him as I soaked in the steaming hot water. As I ran the towel down his arm, I noticed a new tattoo it was an angel with Mother Coco's name underneath, the drawing itself was so beautiful.

"Bae you got a new tat, that's hot."

"Yeah I got it this morning. Rico got the same tattoo with me."

"Well I have a question?" Tyson said preparing to ask me.

"I'm all ears babe," I was laughing.

"I see you have several tattoos yourself but not one of them for me yet, why not?"

"Now you know the answer to this question, and furthermore you don't have any of me either," I said trying to change the conversation and I bite his earlobe.

"That's how you got started last night and didn't finish it."

After our long soak in the tub, we got dressed, got the clothes from the dryer and sat on the sofa to fold the last load of clothes up for Rico.

"So you ready to get back to work," me making conversation

"Yeah I should be getting back to work huh?"

"When you are ready babe, just take your time."

"Maybe tomorrow, let's get these clothes over to Rico's."

We finished packing the clothes up and loading the car.

We made it to Rico and Kinsten's house which was about a 15-minute ride across town, after we have had our herbal tea session, and had sprayed Tyson's Polo Sport. We took the box out the car and headed up to the door, I rang the doorbell, a few moments later Rico answered it.

"Sup big brother, nice to see ya Maine, what you got in the box?"

"I cleaned some clothes and thought about you Ric, now you have some of my style."

"Come on in, I have some people you should meet."

Rico had a smirk on his face. We stepped on inside the door, Tyson held the box as he and Rico headed upstairs, I followed the voices down the short corridor into the family room.

I stood there looking around at Brittney's mom and dad sat on the sofa, Brittney on the loveseat and Kinsten in his recliner with a beer in hand.

"Hello everyone, how are you all doing?" me trying to sound pleasant in a very acquired room, by this time Tyson and Rico had finally joined us in family room, we had a seat beside Brittney.

"Meet Cedric and Maya Warner, Brittney's parents."

They were the owners of a small business right here in town, passed down from generation to generation for over 45 years, this family was very well off and Mrs. Brittney had a lot to live up too with the Warner name.

Much to our surprise Mr. Kinsten Charles Rumble, a graduate from Southern University, and was a lawyer in top law firm in the city, which meant Rico had a great chance in the world.

So I asked.

"How did you two meet with such great and wonderful parents?"

Story goes the Mr. Rumble and Warner's went to the same church, the two of them had met at a revival as friends, that year Rico took Brittney to their winter formal at the church and now they can't stand to not be around each other.

"We trust and love Rico, we know he's a good and decent young man, for our baby girl," said Brittney's mother.

"These two are so focused and we have been trying to keep them that way."

Tyson and the Warner's seemed to hit it off just fine, they also knew Tyson's mother from the church as well, they loved her dearly because she had done so much for the community and the church.

The time was 10:00pm, when we all decide to leave for the night.

In the car Tyson asked me.

"What did I think about the Warner's?"

"They were ok, they were cool bae."

"What do you think about marriage?" which had caught me off guard completely.

"Man, Tyson what are you talking about?"

"I'm just curious that's all Jisain, don't get your hopes up", he said with quotations as he laughed.

"I don't know, I think marriage is something beautiful just to have that blissful lover and friend until death do you part, it's some hot shit and how about you Mr. Jacks, what are your thoughts on the issue?"

"Well maybe I'll show you one day, but I think marriage is the most honorable way a man shows his companion the way he really feels and that he's not ashamed to show God and the world you really love somebody," He had answered perfectly.

"Wow babe that's deep even for you, what's own your mind?" I was very tense by this time.

"I was thinking about mom and daddy's wedding, what it was like, what moms was feeling at the moment she and dad said their vows, did my dad cry, trying to picture mom coming down the aisle, I was wondering if the family was there?"

He wanted to know so much that I got lost in his babbling.

"Babe you're losing me, slow down," I was frantic at this point.

"That's what I wanted from you, look at this."

Taking his hand from pocket as we drove into the driveway, Tyson was proposing, I began to cry gently, staring at his sweet and kind face.

"Baby in the time I've been with you I feel like my life has changed for the better.

You've tested my love over again me and I know God has giving me a gift when he gave me you, my mom loves you, my family loves you, your family adores you, just say the words, either way you got me."

"Yes Ty yes" I watched his face light up as I said the words, I could see he was fighting back his tears. (But one manage to fall down his face)

I know this love was truly real. I was crazy in love, over the hills with this man. God had giving me the man of my dreams, when I thought I would never love again I now finally believed I was truly happy I thanked God that night.

Chapter 11

After a long 2 weeks of the dreaded and painful events and then the trip to Six Flags, Rico and getting engaged I was feeling tired, luckily I still had some time off work, so I went by my apartment to pick up my mail and finally begin packing up my things since I had decided to move in with Tyson in our new home.

I was headed back to the car, when I walked out the door, I ran into my neighbor Carter, heading up to my place.

"Sup Maine, what's going on?"

"I know we just became friends but can I ask you a personal question?" I asked.

"Well I've been good so far, just getting things packed up, Tyson and I are engaged, were moving in together after almost a year of dating, I'm nervous, but were happy."

"Well congrats on the engagement hopefully I'll be there with you guys on the big day bro?"

"Hey are you keeping your place here, maybe y'all can still come by here and we can chill sometime?" Carter asked.

"Yeah I'm keeping it, for now dude, I can't afford to leave here completely," I answered....

I looked around my apartment one last time and I knew in my heart Tyson and I was ready to take that next step in life, I gathered the rest of my bags and headed to the car and pulled off down the road.

But I did keep decide to keep that apartment since I couldn't get out that lease and it was also great to have a place to still come to with all my furniture and things still being here and all....

Chapter 12

After we got inside, Tyson headed for the bedroom for the night, I was sitting in the lazy boy in the bedroom when my phone ring it was Jeffery.

"Hello Jisain?"

"What's up Jeff, I just knew it wouldn't be long before you called me, how are you doing Maine?" I asked.

"Whoa this is a new me, you're all happy and shyt it's been a long while and you sound happy."

"Well I just got focused, and I've been doing a lot of praying to the Lord, it's Him who's working these miracles in my life."

"Well Ji Maine, I had to talk to you, I know you had some good advice, that's why I called you."

"Well get to it Jeff, what is it," I was getting annoyed.

"I think Khadijah is up to something, she's been distant lately and she's not even talking to me, when I do finally get her calls."

"Did you tell her the truth about you being with men Jeffery?"

"Yeah she knows all of that Jisain, that's why I asked you to meet her so there wouldn't be any secrets between us and I think she's pregnant. His voice aching in fear, "My life is a fucking maze, I came to you for some direction," I could hear him beginning to cry.

I dropped the phone in that moment I went into praying mode.

"Dear Lord,

It's me I'm coming to you right now in the standing of a friend that needs now, your comfort and your direction in Jesus name I pray.

Amen"

"Hey Jeff I have to get going, but you call me in a few days take care, where do you work maybe I'll come by and see how you are doing?"

"Oh I work over at the El Dorados, at Sportsman's Paradise."

"Maybe I'll come by for lunch one-day next week."

"Yeah that'll be cool I guess, well goodnight," He said as the line died.

Today was the Presidential Election. The time was 6:18 am, when Tyson had awakened, I could feel him rubbing my face, and he kissed my lips and gently called out to me.

"Good morning my big head, time to get up babe," he said, as he wiped the cold from my eyes.

"Same to you big head," I said.

"It's time to get this Black Man elected into the White House," He said headed down the hallway.

I walked in the bathroom where Tyson was already there relieving himself, so stood waiting for him to finish, I as I stood there relieving myself, Tyson grabbed a handful of my ass, I smiled.

"Baby we don't have the time to miss around, we got to be at the polls in a minute and we both have to go to work," me being a tease.

"Later tonight we can handle that," Tyson making his piece jump.

"Oh yeah you know that babe," I answered pushing my ass against his piece.

I flushed and we started to get dressed.

"Tyson you know we have to start planning the wedding, when, where, the guests you know all that stuff, so lunch you, me later at El Dorados 1:30 and don't be late".

"Yeah that's a bet babe."

We headed out the door at 6:49, shortly after we made our way to the designated voter's office at the local school. There was no line so we were in and out. I dropped Tyson off at his car and I was on my way to work. When I got to work to what seemed to be an endless pile of letters from people who needed so much advice, but there was one letter that came across my desk, to my surprise it was from Carter.

It read...

Dear Mr. Styles,

I'm having some problems with my lover. We've been arguing a lot about the way I've been behaving when I'm not around. I love him but I can't help it that I cheat on him with the other guys.

I've been caught up in some shit behind my so called friends who went back and gave him a full report of all the dirty naughty details.

He bust the windows out my car, slashed my 22's, and he even took all the pictures in the apartment and set them all on fire in a mad rage, I got the fire out before spread, Maine just give me the basics.

Carter the Cheater

It was my civil duty to do the good work and respond to the reader of my column but I was a bit skeptical, because this was my friend so I gave it my best shot.

Dear Carter,

It seems to me that you have a severe case of what I like to call "Varityitis." You can't get enough of what you want, and when what you need is right in front of your eyes and probably has been there for some time.

You say you love this guy and you seem to have an ounce of guilt for your madness, they've obviously have found out and now you're reaping what you sowed, or what we call that lady name Karma.

This is what you did, you have to take responsibility, you go to him and you work this out, you guys sit down and talk and you listen very closely to what he says to you, it's going to determine if he's in or out.

Just pray to God that he forgives you and that's it's not too late to make things right.

God Bless,

Mr. Styles

When I finished responding to the letter for the column, I could see my phone flashing, it was a text message, it was Tyson saying he was going to meet at lunch that he would meet me in the lobby of the casino. Replied to the message and grabbed my keys and headed out the door.

I was only a few minute away from the casino so there was no rush. I pulled in the entrance, the valet gave me a ticket, and I headed inside to the lobby. I saw Tyson sitting there on a bench looking so damn good in his work uniform.

He greeted me and we waited to be seated, when to our surprise, there was Jeffery. He was going to be our server. He seated us and took our drink orders.

His face was bit broken to see us sitting there so intimately.

"Welcome to Sportsman's, hey Ji I see you didn't waste time huh?"

"Yeah my finance' is getting me lunch and this is close to my work you know," I answered.

"Your finance', so your engaged?"

"Yeah His Finance'" Tyson's voice echoed across the room.

"What can get for you gentlemen this fine evening?" (His face was very much screwed up he was very mad.)

"We'll both have the Philly cheesesteak sandwich thank you," Tyson was acting very stand offish at this point.

"And your drinks," He added. "I'll have a Sprite and he will have a Coke."

Jeffery walked off slowly, placed our orders and walked off the floor, about a minute or five later another server, named Julius, said he was talking over the table he placed our drinks on the table and went to check on our order.

"Ok so you got me here, let's talk about the wedding, have you been thinking about anything," Tyson was calming down.

I took a couple of deep breathes before I spoke.

"Well here's what I been thinking so far, we could have a small ceremony over at the house 25 to 50 guests, the colors are white, black and blue our favorite colors.

Big cake made by my girl Lena's grandmother Mrs. Tammy, we are wearing white tuxedos blue shirts with the black tie or bowtie and flowers everywhere, very soft music, candles lite everywhere, we honeymoon in Philadelphia, get our Marriage Certificate and paperwork done," I said out of breath.

"Everything sounds good, damn well you seemed to have figured this shit out huh bae?" Tyson asked.

"Well how much is this going to cost us this big question?" he added.

"Well about $2500 to $3000 racks babe."

His face dropped, "Are you fucking serious?" he burst out laughing.

"Okay if that's what you want you got it."

When our food finally came, we sat and ate, when Tyson said, he had a surprise for me, he said he wanted to wait for later but the time was right, he took the box from his pocket and gave it to me, it was a Gold Bracelet, it was engraved with our initials, I handed it to him and he placed it in my wrist.

"Bae sup?" I said as he placed the bracelet on my wrist.

"Just giving you a sample of how things are gonna be since were going to be making this permanent."

Soon after we had finished lunch, Tyson paid the check, I left the tip and we headed back to work.

Tyson walked me out to valet, his face was so full of joy and he did the craziest and funniest thing, when we got outside there was a crowd of people standing around, when he lays a kiss on me in front of a group of strangers and I was too shocked for words say the least, that I burst out laughing.

"Babe are you okay," I asked looking at him with this very confused look on my face.

"Yeah I am just, you've made me so damn happy, I'm getting married, all of this is real for me now," I was laughing harder.

Tyson gave me the warmest hug squeezing me so hard.

We walked out the door and I got into my car and drove back to work.

When I got back to work, I was sitting in my office at the desk thinking to myself about what was about to take place with me and my future and I had the perfect idea, I could announce our engagement in the paper, but I thought no that's not the way I wanted to make this announcement.

I finished up the rest of my letters for the advice column and at 5:00 I was leaving for the office for the day.

I got to the house and I had a plan to pamper my babe tonight. I got in the kitchen and cooked us up a huge dinner baked chicken, mashed potatoes, green beans, cornbread, and even baked chocolate cake.

I cleaned the house and ran him a hot bubble bath and lite candles all over the house.

By the time he came walking through the door. I was wearing his robe, my body was fresh and smelled divine from the Phat Farm body spray on his robe. He walked over to me kiss my lips and took the beer from my hand.

> "Welcome home Mister, the night is officially set now that you're here, I've ran you a bath and your dinner is ready so what's first me or the meal?"

> "Now you know what I want the most is that meal." Then he laughs!

> "No baby it's you?"

I began to strip him out of his painted on clothes and he still smelled like a worn out work boot. I immediately began kissing his sexy skin, he wrapped his arms around me and we walked to the bubble bath.

He undressed me from his robe and we stepped in the tub me sitting in his lap, he began wiping me down with the luffa, first from my back then down to my lower back with his strong hands massaging my neck I heard him ask.

> "Baby what was wrong with you at lunch today," with his head on my shoulder?

"Oh Tyson I am good just happy with everything going on and you caught me off guard with the gift."

Once the water had gotten cold, we got dressed in our boxer shorts and muscle shirts. We sat down to dinner in front of the tele and watched the rest of the presidential election.

Obama was in the led with 250 votes needing 20 votes to win the election and for a second we were beginning to think things wouldn't work out for Obama, but 20 minutes later it flashed across the screen Barack Obama your new presidential elect.

We jumped to our feet and begin to run around the house sliding across the floors screaming and praising Jesus. It seems the people had spoking. A moment in life history, our 1st Black president, the first ever!

We were so excited about the news that we fell asleep on the couch in front of the television in each other's arms knowing that life itself was taking a new turn, not just for us but for American also!

Chapter 13

Once the elections were over there seem to be a change in streets out in the city and around the country, the news seem to be getting good some days, bad other days.

For the next few months at work I've seen some of the craziest shit. People were being so cheerful for the holidays to violent in the worst ways. Everyone had high spirits except for the article being printed all over President Barack Obamas every move and his plans to better the economy, healthcare and taxes.

Thanksgiving was just around the corner and Tyson and I had finally planned the wedding date for June 15 of the New Year to save us a lot of headaches. I even got an updated letter from Carter this is what he said.......

Dear Mr. Styles,

I took your advice I sat down with my lover. He told me some things that made me think he said that in spite of all the shit I've put him through he was not giving up on me.

He wants me to do right and that we're going to try and work it out. He even went to see my mom and spilled the beans about everything, my mom went to my grandmother and she even spilled the beans.

They all trapped me in the house about a week ago and told me off and man that shit was crazy. I actually felt so bad I went to church that Sunday and I broke down.

I came home I grabbed my babe and I told him that I was sorry for all that shit and from that moment I was going to start doing right by him.

Thanks for your advice, man it's really helping me make some changes.

You take care,

Carter

I sat there for a full second and I thought to myself that this was too good to see, someone really took my advice, and it was inspiring and so humbling to help someone get their break through.

I had a knock at the door it was my manager Mr. Marcus Moon, he came in and sat down at my desk.

"Hey Mr. Styles, I know it's only been a nine months since you've started with us, but I've been watching your progress and I wanted to personally give you the news, that you are being promoted here at The Times.

You are getting a raise, 5 dollars more, that was great news to get on the job."

"I need Sundays off for church, each and every Sunday!"

"Yes sure you got it no problem" Answered Marcus.

It was about time for me to get home. I was on my way out the door, when I got a call from my sister. She said that she found out she a two-week vacation and if I needed her to call, and, she wanted something to eat so I stopped off to get her some Subway, that's what she needed I felt in that moment.

I swung by her house to take her the food she kissed me on my cheek and I was on my way.

On the road home, I started thinking a lot about was this marriage life, was it really what I wanted for myself? It has been a long time since I met someone that really took my breath away.

He dries my every tear away when I cry, and I know somewhere deep inside that we are supposed to be together. I felt like he was a second chance, sent by the man above himself that I really truly love.

I was happier with him that I'd ever be in all my life with someone like Tyson.

I drove up to see mom and dad, I sat at their feet.

"Hey I miss you guys so much there's so much to tell. Well my job gave me a raise, and I wanted to tell you guys something, (I took a deep breath), I've met someone and I want you guys to know that I love him!

Mommy you remember the way you felt about dad, that's how I feel and so much more! We've been dating for about a year, I met his mother, she pasted away a few months ago, and you guys are going to love Mrs. Coco!

Tell her I said hello and that Tyson finally proposed and we've set a date, we're getting married! I never thought all of this would be happening to me without you guys being here to share all these wonderful fulfilling moments that life has given us.

I had tears in my eyes, showing them my ring. Dad I know you are turning in your grave right now, but I want you to know I'm happy just the way I am.

I got your names tattooed on both of my shoulders, dad Tyson is a good man, you and mom would be so proud of him. He's helped my heart heal from past relationship. I just wish you could meet him. He's smart, sweet, he's a warm soul that really cares and adores me, and he is who I wanted in a lover.

What I admire the most about him is he's strong just like you dad. He holds me down when I feel like letting go and he prays me through the tough times. I have to go, I have so much to do I love you guys so much later".

I got in the car and headed to house where he was waiting for me. When I pulled up at the house, Tyson's car was there in the driveway. I parked the car and went inside. I could smell dinner had already been cooked. I cook hear water running.

"Babe how was your day?"

"It was good, I got a promotion."

"I'll be out in a minute," Tyson said as I was looking around the kitchen.

I could hear him in the bedroom getting dressed. He finally came in the kitchen.

> "Congratulations babe I heard it on the voicemail, so I cooked your dinner to celebrate."

We sat and ate dinner, after we had finished dinner, Tyson and I cleaned the dishes, he washed them, and I dried them and we called it a night.

The today was my birthday, I had to work, but I didn't mind, everyone at work pitched in and got me a gift. I decided to take the rest of the day off just to go and hang out and celebrate.

I went shopping and got a haircut just to enjoy myself. Later that evening when I got home, Tyson's car wasn't in the driveway, I went inside, the lights were off and there it was.

> "Surprise happy birthday Jisain"

Everyone was there, my best friend Lena and her son Kenny did the decorations, Lucy cooked the food and Carter and Lee even had my cake.

> "So what do you give to the man who has everything," asked Tyson.

> "There's nothing I really don't need, I have my babe and all my friends and family are here, I feel so blessed," I explained.

We partied that night, drinks were flowing, everyone was eating and having a great time, it was the best, and we even did karaoke. Around 11:30 everyone took me in the kitchen, they sat me at the table, Tyson walked in with my favorite cake, it was Cookies and Cream with Oreo's in the frosting, the cake even had my picture on it, I loved it, he lite the candles and everyone gathered around the table. Tyson sang the happy birthday song, his voice was dry and he was awful because he had been drinking but it was still lovely that he tried, I was a mess, and the tears began to run down my face.

I looked around at everyone waiting for me to make a wish. I took a deep breath and blew out the candles. He kissed my cheek and both my hands. I cut the cake, served some to my guests and we began cleaning the house, before everyone left for the night.

I looked at the gifts that were sitting one the in the living room. Tyson read the names to me as I opened my gifts from everyone. I got outfits from everyone. Carter got me this fly rainbow tie that I adored. But the best gift came from Tyson.

It was a gift bag with a teddy bear dressed like a Dallas Cowboy football player, a bottle of Dolce' and Cabana , a birthday card, and a Coach wallet with his picture inside and many other gadgets.

"Hey babe, how about Christmas day?"

"For the wedding?"

"It feels right and I like that date and this will be the most special day for us," I explained.

"So what's next?"

"We have to be fitted for our tuxes and did you write your vows yet?"

"Yes and I can't wait until you hear them."

Chapter 14

Thanksgiving was about a week away. Tyson and I were on a rampage getting things together for dinner and that fast approaching wedding. Today we were leaving from the tux fitting, as we walked out the door, to the car. Tyson spotted his ex, as he walked passed the Tuxedo shop.

"Tristan, what's going on Bruh," he said, as he tightened his grip on my shoulder.

"Dice, what's going on, wow this is a surprise," he was surprised to see him.

"2 things, I haven't gone by Dice since high school and 2nd I want you to meet someone, this is Jisain, my fiancé," Tyson was looking me in my eyes at that point.

"How you doing love, I'm Tristan," sounding quite happy with his voice in all high pitched, guess he was surprised about the news.

"Well Tyson, Jisain isn't half bad at all, you've done a great job,"

"No," I said cutting him off "I've done a wonderful job with this man, and he's a fantastic part of my life, you should know right," I said throwing shade.

"Well we must be going, we have a lot thing to do, Tyson you are going invite Tristan to the wedding aren't you?" I asked the smirk on my face was priceless.

"If you can make it, will save you a seat, just keep your eyes in the paper for more information," I added.

In the car, I was making calls, the cake was ordered, the only things left on the list of things to do, were the house decorations and meeting with Tyson's pastor, his name was Cedric Parker.

Pastor Parker was over a small church on the outside of town. Tyson knew Pastor Parker from his mother speaking so highly of him over the years. We sat down with Pastor Parker, he and Tyson were catching up about thing's he had missed over the last few months from Mother Coco's passing away to us getting engaged.

Tyson asked, "Would he preside over our wedding it was going to be held at our house."

Pastor Parker said, "He would be honored, but under the circumstances that we start attending services a bit more regular on Sunday's."

With the wedding planning finally behind us, the only thing left was our guest list and the announcement, once we were inside. We sat down and got to thinking.

"Okay Jisain 50 guests, you have 25 and I have 25.

"Yes just 50, but these guests are out of a question right now."

"Let's make a list then Jisain", Tyson was getting antsy.

"Okay! Well I know my sister Lucy and Darion are coming with my niece," I said.

"Oh Okay other than them and Rico, maybe Brittney, if her parents say it okay, who else?" Tyson asked.

"Well Carter and Lee can be our Best Men, and Rico and Brittney can be the Ring bearer and Flower girl and my friend Lucy will be my Madrid of Honor," I had come up with some of the bridal party.

"Of course your family, my family, and our friends from work," Tyson said.

Done with all the wedding talk, we began planning the Thanksgiving dinner.

We went in the kitchen and got to cooking. I had the dressing, ham, potato salad and the cornbread casserole. Tyson was working on the Turkey, the Brisket, the Bar Be Qu, and Baked Beans. We even did several dozen Deviled Eggs and 2 Strawberry Cheesecakes.

Once we had the meal all cooked up and everything was wrapped up in the fridge, Tyson and I headed for the couch, where he laid his head across my legs, turned on his side, he was rubbing my leg with his hands, it seemed to be strange at 1st but I was starting feel curious about his behavior this night since, his mom had passed way.

"Baby", he said, calling out to me.

"Yeah Babe talk to me"

"It's been a long time since I've had fun just cooking and laughing."

"So why do you sound so sad?"

"That was me and moms thing", his voice had dropped down two octaves, "She would cook and sing all around the house here, I'd come home for the holiday's", he said very dry like.

"Hey let me tell you something, your mom hears your cries and I know she wishes she could be here with you bae, but she had to go when the Lord called.

Look when my parents died, I never thought God will bless me with someone I could pour all the love I had inside for them. I want you to know something, if you ever feel sad or afraid, just think of the love you have for your mom's and pray for peace."

We fell asleep on the sofa, like two wild kittens fighting for a sock.

Today was Thanksgiving. I had been in bed all morning after a long night of tasseling on the couch with Tyson. When, I was awakened by a sound so sweet. My eyes were still in the dizzy state, I looked around the room Tyson was coming around to my side of the bed with breakfast, he was singing so sweetly.

"Good morning my bro, Happy Thanksgiving, are you ready to eat and I'll be watching the game, it's about to start in a minute, I'm ready to see my Boys Kick Ass," he was excited.

It was very strange how happy he was, I sat in bed, stunned. While we were eating, I ate very slowly, studying his every move. He was dressed and ready for the day and it was only 9:30, so I stopped him.

"You are too damn happy what's up Bae?"

"Well you said that we were going to Philadelphia for our honeymoon, I changed all that, and I hope you are okay with me because I just booked and paid for our trip, we are going on a cruise to the Bahamas," He said.

I've been working it on for some time now and they just confirmed this morning, we will be leaving New Year's Day, newlyweds hand in hand."

I grabbed him and kissed his cheek, "You're a beautiful man, you are so sweet and romantic to me," I was gushing like a volcano.

"Wait, what about our marriage license?"

"Let's just worry about the wedding and the trip Bahamas and we can deal with that when we get back," He answered.

Once I finally got dressed, we headed into kitchen, to warm up the food for the game when we got a call from Carter he was inviting us to the house, we gathered the food, loaded it into the car and in the trunk and headed over to Carter's new house, he had moved out to other side of town about three months ago.

When we arrived at his spot, there were cars everywhere. There was barely a place to park.

I knocked on the door, Lee answered, he came out to the car and helped gathered the food to bring it inside to the kitchen. When we went inside there were people everywhere sitting around shouting Happy Thanksgiving, it felt like home, we headed into the kitchen and made space for the for the rest of the food, that's where Carter was.

"What's up Jisain, Tyson, good to see you guys made it, thanks for bringing the food, friends in there, and the blunt smokers are in my bedroom, and y'all make yourselves at home?"

"Well could you lead us to your bedroom, we had something good you'd want to try," Tyson insisted.

Carter had great taste, his room colors was Brown and Gold, with a lot of Movie Posters he had collected over the years, he had a nice bedroom and there even was a loveseat over in the corner. We sat on the loveseat, while Tyson took the 2 blunt from his shirt pocket, lighting one and sent it into rotation.

When we were finally at our full potential it was time to eat so we all headed for the kitchen where all the delicious food was waiting Tyson offered to fix my plate and I was cool with it. When everyone was finally served we all stood around and said Grace

We joined hands and Carter led the blessing.

"Dear Lord,

We come giving you thanks for the many blessing, you saw fit for us to make it over, for your grace and mercy, for the time you have allowed us to have.

For our new President Barack Obama, he's going to change our country, for the meal prepared here, for the gift of family, friends, and fellowship.

For the meal that we are about to receive in our bodies for strength, nourishment and health for another day's journey under your grace mercy and care

In your strong and powerful name I pray,

Amen."

We sat around the huge family room, watching the Cowboys play on the 64' big screen, the game was just about over and the Cowboys were down by a touchdown, when Romo scored the win point winning the game.

We sat around for the next few hours, chilling, drinking, and smoking bud until around 11:00, then we headed down to Club Phoenix, it was crazy Tyson won the dance contest, and received a free drink and 25 dollars.

I decided to stay reserved tonight because one of us had to drive home and Tyson was beyond drunk when we left the club at 3a.m.

I held him up as we made our way to the car, when Tyson began throwing up, his breath smelled like stale pizza and he was quite weak. Once he was strapped in the car, I got in on the driver side and headed home.

When we got home, I sat with Tyson in the shower until we were fresh and clean, I dressed him in his boxer shorts and a t-shirt, I dressed myself and I got in bed, laying there I was thinking about the day as I drifted off to sleep.

Chapter 15

The wedding was about 3 and half weeks away and everything was just about done except the announcement. I set an appointment to take pictures with my friends. It was set for the December 4th at Target.

I called everyone and gave them the information. Carter had not been fitted for his tux, so I told him I'd go with him so he could get fitted.

When I arrived at work, it seemed to a breath of fresh air, from all the wedding talk, at my desk were flowers, candy, and gift wrapped up in a big blue bow and card, I sat down and opened the card it was from Tyson he had written me a nice love note....

> Say their love, how you been, me I'm just perfectly fine, now that I've encountered you, your light, your love has beamed me up and shot me away beyond my wildest dreams, and you have taught me that love over comes pain, I'm sane, I'm saved, and I'm free to be all the man you need.
>
> XO, Tyson

Work went just great after my surprise, I got to the column to try and gave the readers what I could them my advice to their many letters.

Around 11:30, I got a call, they said it was a strange guy on line 1, I picked up the line.

"Hello this is Jisain, and how can I help you today."

"Yes this is Tristian, I just wanted to talk to you and let you know something Tyson is not the man you think he is?"

I sat the phone on the receiver placing it on the speakerphone. I was texting Tyson letting him know Tristian was on the line.

"I believe that was only with you, from what I was told" I replied.

"You're just some bitter boy who's jealous of losing your man" I added.

"Well if I'm so jealous look for yourself, I know you can down there where you work," he said.

I hung up the line, and I sat back in my chair, thinking about what he had said and what had just happened.

I got on Google, typed in Tyson's full name, and there was a mugshot of him.

About 2 years ago he was arrested for assault and took anger management and that was it. I printed the information and placed it in a manila folder and sat it on my desk. I headed out to lunch. I drove down to El Dorado's for some Gumbo and rice. I was sitting at the bar, waiting for my bags, when Jeffery came over and sat with me.

We talked for a while and I told him what I had found out about Tyson.

"I felt like Tyson and I have been on course and with this information I was starting to 2nd think him."

Jeffery was right to the point with me.

"Jisain, you keep moving forward with him, it seems to me that your mind is made up, and you need to go talk to Tyson and get to the bottom of things."

I got my lunch and I decided to head over to the construction site where Tyson worked.

I parked the car and went inside the building, there was a young lady at the desk name Tatianna Simpson, and she appeared to be about 25 years old.

"Hello is Tyson Jacks here."

"Uh no, he's not here, he's working at a site right now, but you could leave a message."

"No love that's okay," I said, turning to head out the door.

As I got in the car, I saw his car was still there, I sat there in the car and started going over everything in my head and I came to the conclusion that well we got our thing going and this talk about his past would just get in the way.

I headed back to work and for some odd reason I still couldn't eat, I left my Gumbo in the car and headed back to my office. In my office to my surprise was Carter.

"Mr. Styles, you work here nigga," he asked.

"Yeah, it's been a little while now," as I was sitting in my chair.

"So when I wrote in to the advice column, it was you, I was writing to?" his eyes were big in his head as he made the statement.

"Yeah, so I already knew all about you and Lee but I was doing my job."

"So what are you doing here Maine," I asked?

"Well you said something about going to get fitted for a tux, I was ready to go make it happened."

"I don't get off work for another few hours, but I can call them and let them know you're coming."

"Ok Jisain cool and I wanted to let you know, I broke up with Lee and it was fucked up Maine," he explaining.

He was fighting back tears as strong as he was, but I could see that things were going down from there.

"We were talking and he told me that he was done with our relationship and that he would be gone in a few days, but I've moved on Maine, I'm just chilling for a little while."

"Well in the short time I've got to know you, I know you'll bounce back, I know you'll be cool," I was trying to cheer him up.

"You get down to the Tuxedo shop and get fitted, I just sent you the address to your phone, they'll be expecting you," I added.

"Just call me after you get things straighten out, sometime tomorrow Carter," I walked him out to the lobby.

"Yeah Maine, I'll shake back, I'll get at cha, when I get done with the fitting."

My work load was just as light as the day had been, I was finally choosing a beautiful font to do the wedding announcement ad for the paper, printed the pages for the paper and got things turned in before I left for the day.

Meanwhile, Tyson had just got off work and was heading to pick-up Rico for his tux fitting.

At the tuxedo shop, Rico was in the middle of his fitting when Carter came in for his fitting and the manager was expecting him.

"Carter sup Maine," Tyson said, greeting him with a hand shack.

"We just about to leave, just getting lil' bro a fixed-up you know?" he added, as they paid the rental fee at the counter.

"Oh yeah, sup bro, I just came from Jisain's office, he sent me right on over," Carter said.

"Yeah and tomorrow we all are meeting at Target for the photo for the ad in the paper, it's at 4:00, if you can make it," he said to Carter on the way out the door, "Just call Jisain's phone".

"Yeah, you got it," Carter answered.

"Then tomorrow, 4:00 sharp, Target, we out Maine," as they were out the door.

Carter was fitted for his tux for the wedding on the way out he got a call from the guy he had met at the club name Lucas, asking could they get together and talk.

Carter said, "Yeah they could."

Carter was on his way to meet Lucas, he stayed in the fancy part of town, Golden Meadows, he drove up to a white house on St. Johns Ave, and calling Lucas as he pulled up in the driveway.

Lucas was 5'7, slim build, a red bone cutie with a nice smile and went to Southwood High School, the pretty boy types you know.

He came out and sat in the passenger seat of Carter's ride and they were off, heading to meet us at our place.

They seemed to be hitting off just cool, Lucas was from Florida. His dad had transferred to the Air Force Base here down to the south. He went Southern Universality and was about 26.

They pulled up to our house, honking the horn and Tyson went out to greet them. I was in the kitchen when they came inside, Carter helped me gathered the drinks and snacks

Carter said "Jisain I think he might be the one".

They met about 4 months while he and Lee's thing was still coming to a close and that's his babe Lucas, I was guessing he was special.

We finally joined Tyson and Lucas, we're rolling some herb for us to smoke and enjoy.

We were sitting enjoying ourselves, I got down to business to putting this Lucas in the hot seat, asking a series of questions, to get a feel for who he was, but he was sharp he told.

"I'm a strong, young, pretty prep boy and I'm about my coins."

Tyson just handed the pieces of my face that had shattered on the floor. Well his impression was set with me, I thought Carter had him a natural bad ass and he dug Lucas.

We were having such a great time that before it was time to take it in, the photoshoot was tomorrow and we needed to look well rested in those photos.

We walked Carter and Lucas to the door and I slipped a note in Carters pockets and bid them a farewell.

We locked up the house and got cleaned up for bed. We cleaned the family room and finally we headed to bed Tyson said a short prayer and drifted on the stars off to our dreams.

Chapter 16

Beep, beep, beep the alarm clock was going off and it was going to be busy day. The time was already 9:30 and Tyson and I were tangled up in bed.

We took our time to get up but we did finally get up 30 minutes later. We got dressed in the most comfortable cloths we could find and headed out the door at 10:30, in the car, Tyson seemed to be still sleepy, so we made a quick stop a Mickey D's for a light breakfast and some coffee.

Rico and Brittney were in school which meant we would have had to have to wait for them and meet them later that day.

We drove over to the Boardwalk and walked around for a little while. We went in Rue 21, looking at some t-shirts, Tyson found a yellow shirt that had some crazy designs and even a matching blue shirt for me.

I found some nice fitted jeans and Tyson found some jean shorts, we made our way to the counter, paid for our items and we headed over to the Nike store looking for shoes.

In the store, we ran into Jeffery and to our surprise a very pregnant girlfriend Khadijah, she was a beautiful young girl, Jeffery's face was in utter shock.

"Hi Jisain, what's going on?"

"Well, well, well," Tyson was in a giggling fizz.

"Just out with my bae' shopping," I was looking at Tyson with such horror and my stomach was in knots, wanting to laugh.

"Hey keep your eyes in the paper next week, our wedding announcement will be in the living section ads, we are so excited, you guys be well and take care."

Tyson grabbing my hand, "Well we have to be going, he wanted to look at shoes, before the photoshoot but good luck with your baby and everything how many months are you, Mama?"

"Oh I'm, she's 3 months," Jeffery said cutting her off.

"Well y'all have a good time but we have to be going," Tyson was rushing them off.

Tyson rushed me down the nearest aisle, he looked around then he gave me the most passionate kiss.

He grabbed these ugly pair of Jordan's, they were gold, silver, and blue and he was obsessed with them that he got us both a pair.

After shopping, we decided to go to the movies. The Biggie Smalls film was showing at Regal Court and we wanted to watch. The film was good Derek Luke was an okay Diddy and they told the story very well, which was not easy at all with all their drama.

Tyson sat with his arm around my neck, my leg in his lap it was a great let your hair down moment. He would rap songs from the movie, in my ear that made me smile and we had a great time at the movie.

After the movies, it was time to get everyone all together to get dressed before we went to the photoshoot. Rico and Brittney were getting ready, and then were being dropped off at the Target. Carter was on the way and my sis was putting on her final touches on before she made her way to our house.

We were on Youree Dr. and Southfield about to drive through the light, when Tyson showed me the billboard, it read....

I'M GETTING MARRIED, OFFICAILY OFF THE MARKET, it was a special moment to know he did that, to surprise me and it was signed with his name.

At Target, we headed back to meet with our Photographer name Joshua Perez. He took us back where Tyson, the family and I could choose the same background for the photos, and we choose 3 backgrounds.

 A blue background with flowers all around us, the next one was a park background with a bench and the last one was all white.

In the blue background with the flowers, we stood right in the middle of Rico and Brittney to his right was my sister and then finally Carter his snapped 3 shots.

He then changed to the background in the park, I sat on the bench between my sis and Brittney, while, Rico, Tyson, and Carter were standing behind us with their hand on our shoulder.

The final picture was a simple picture of Tyson and I standing back to back, with our heads touching and our eyes closed, not looking in the camera.

Once we were done with the shoot, we sat around looking at the samples as they came out to choose the pictures we liked.

Joshua said it would be a week before the pictures would be ready.

We dropped off the kids and we drove home, hung the tuxedoes in the closet and I went to take a shower just to rinse off, and I stepped out the shower, body still steamy hot. I ran in the room for the body lotion.

"Damn baby, I got you right back there I see."

"Yeah you did babe, but uh I got you right too, "I was flirting.

Tyson walked over to me, sitting me on the dresser, and began playing with my wet body all over his boxers, and his hands all over my ass, it just made me so fucking hot.

I wrapped my legs around his waist, my hands around his neck, he carried me over to our bed holding me tight, today felt so special, and we decided to flip each other.

Tyson went down playing in my love, tasting my juices making me moan and biting my lip, I could feel my toes curl as his tongue push deeper in my surface and that shit drove me so fucking crazy, he would look up at me and it was like telepathy I could feel his thoughts.

Once he was done with my pleasure, it was his turn I flipped him over, laying him on his chest. I took his nature and tasted it, stroking him in my mouth I could hear him saying.

"Baby, do that trick with your tongue on my shit."

I tickled him with my tongue just along the shaft, he was losing his mind, and I knew it was on.

Tyson placed me on my side, I felt his nature on my surface, once he was safe inside, he was stroking slow and deep with his finger in mouth, and his other hand on my waist.

He had me where he wanted, he made love so sweetly, I moaned with every long stroke. I could hear him saying.

"I love that shit Jisain, that shit so good babe, throw that ass back on your Daddy dick babe."

I was melting in the purest nirvana. He was so gentle, strong and steady, kissing on my neck, all I could say was.

"I love it too, yes give me that Daddy dick bae", as he wrapped me up his arms around my shoulders, I could feel his heart pounding in his chest, his breath was on my neck, it was so long and strong, I could feel me about to climax.

I was screaming, "Harder" as he was beating me down with his nature, and then I explode in ecstasy, as I was trembling.

I could hear Tyson saying "Babe that ass is so tight, I want some more, don't let me go," as he held me to him, moaning louder. "Yeah baby take your Daddy dick," with his hands squeezing my ass, he was kissing my chest, pushing his love deeper inside my surface as I climbed on top.

"I love you" seemed to be our script while we making sweet love, the sweat between us were sweet, like candy rain.

He was reaching his climax, he pulled out, shooting his juices all over my body, he laid down right there on top, wrapping me up in his arms, and it was unbelievable. We felt so fulfilled.

Chapter 17

"Baby wake up, were late!!"

Tyson already running in a fritz, I jumped in the shower, and I ran in the closet to get dressed.

"What are we late for," I asked?

"Service, baby we're going to be late for church, you forgot too I see," he said.

30 minutes later we were on our way to church. Pastor Parker service was outstanding, the praise and worship was incredible.

After the service was over, we ran into some of everyone, Carter and Lucas, out in the parking lot we even ran into Jeffery and Khadijah.

In the car we decided to have Chinese for lunch over at the Gold Dragon, Carter and Lucas decided to follow us over to the restaurant. We got us a table and went for the buffet, sat at the table and began eating and talking.

Lucas asked, "Was I ready for the wedding?"

I was grinning as I looked into Tyson's eyes and just staring at him, without saying a word for about 2 minutes, with an awkward silence, I finally answered.

"Yes I am definitely ready, I am in love with him, with all my heart and I think, no I know this is what to do."

Tyson kissed my hand and we ate on. Carter and Tyson began talking about there was any talk of a bachelor party, so I brought it up.

"How do gays have a bachelor party?"

"No, Babe I was thinking we could do something small at the house with our family, friends and us that all I need," Tyson said.

I was blushing redder than I ever had.

Carter and Lucas were talking and they realized they had so much in common. We paid for dinner and we were on our way.

At the house we were changing cloths, when this weird vibe took over the house. Tyson was sitting there with his head in his hands, I went over to him.

"What's up babe, Tyson what's wrong, what's on your mind baby?"

"I don't know babe, I'm just feeling weird, like something doesn't want us to get married?"

"Baby listen to me, I want you to think about what you're saying, are you having second thoughts about us, about the wedding?"

"What's it called wedding jitters babe?"

"Yeah, that's it", he said.

"Look at me, look at me and tell me right now, are you sure you want to do this, if you're not ready, I'm okay either way but just know this will be a very expensive party?" I asked. He was trying to cheer him up.

He took a deep breath, smiled and said, "Jisain that's what I needed and I'm so fucking happy you said that, either way we're cool as long as were together."

Feeling reassured we sat in the bed, we were just about to lay down for a nap, when the phone rang, it was Jeffery, he was at the hospital, there was an accident a car hit him on the passenger side, hitting Khadijah and she lost the baby, he was screaming to the top of his lungs in shock.

"We have to go right now, I was putting on my grey Jordan's and I'll explain everything in the car."

When we got to the hospital, we walked in looking for Jeffery and Khadijah, once we found the room, Jeffery was sitting in the hall on the floor bent over, when he looked up at us, his face was covered in tears, and he was still crying a peaceful but sad cry.

Tyson stood him up and gave him a hug.

"1ST off, brother to brother, I'm sorry for your loss Maine, there's no other way to say it.

I just lost my moms, so I know how you feel.

You wanted your baby, Jisain told me you did, to keep it safe and give it all the love a father should, for that I say God Bless you Maine."

I walked over to look at him.

"Look I shouldn't be here, but I do understand what you're going through. Now you pull yourself together and go to her and see about her, she needs you more than ever right."

Shortly after Jeffery cleaned his face, we went in the room to visit with Khadijah was lying there sleeping peacefully, I went over to her side, and I took her hand and spoke this prayer.......

"Dear Lord,

Right now we come to you asking for comfort, peace and understanding for their baby, Khadijah and Jeffery.

The road ahead is gone be tough but you help smooth out, give their hearts, minds, and spirits true joy.

In Jesus name

Amen."

We headed back into the hall. I asked Jeffery if he wanted to smoke, we said he was welcome to join as we were heading to the elevator.

He was actually leaving to go home so he decided to join us.

In the car Tyson and I were rolling blunts while Jeffery lay out across the back seat. I lite a blunt, took a few puffs and gave it to Tyson.

He pulled a few times then handed it over to Jeffery. Tyson lite the other blunt pulls on it a few time then hands it over to me starting a rotation.

"So Jeff what are you going to do, what are you thinking right now?" Tyson asked.

"Well right now I don't know, but I do know that I've got to get away from this pain in my life. Since we got together it's been so much shit, we fight all the time and even today this accident we were fighting then.

I ran a light, this truck came from out of know where and that's when it happened and I was shocked, I'm numb and getting kind of neutral but I'll be alright Maine, y'all just pray for me."

After the smoke break, I told Jeffery to call us in few days' we could do lunch sometime, just right before we drove off.

When we got home, I was so loaded, and I was unable to direct myself. Tyson took my hand, and led me inside the house as my guide, and we headed in for the bedroom and lay in bed.

That night I dreamed about the wedding, it was Jeffery at the altar for me, when Tyson busts in stole my hand and we runaway together.

Chapter 18

The night seemed to drag out. I woke up staring at the wall, Tyson's arm around my waist.

I got up and headed to the kitchen for that bottle of Red Wine that was chilling in the freezer, I poured me a glass and went and had a seat the living room. I sat on the sofa, taking sips from the glass and a voice calling to me.

Tyson was coming down the hallway calling out for me. I sat up when he finally was standing the in my view, I looked up at him taking another sip from the glass.

"Sup baby, I'm just sitting here having a drink and thinking about somethings, you go back to bed."

He came and laid his head on my lap in fetal position, rubbing his hand up and down my leg, he reached up and taking the glass from my hand, taking a few sips himself.

"Yeah I hear you boo and I want you to know you don't have to think about any of that."

"That's why I'm here baby, to hold you through the hard times, dry your tears when you cry, and give you all the love you deserve, you don't have to worry about a thing, I love you, now come to daddy I know how to make you feel better," He said reassuring me.

Tyson grabbed us a blanket from the hall closet, and we stretched out on the living room carpet, with pillows from the sofa, and we wrapped up in it. Tyson was holding onto me tighter than he ever did this night, I fell asleep knowing my baby loved me and I was in pure peace.

The next morning, I was on my way to work, when I got in my chair, I got the stack of letters to read for the column and got to work, before I got down to work I said a silent prayer to myself and then I got down to business putting the advice column together.

I got a call from Target, the pictures were ready for pick up, I told them I'd be there or that I'd see if Tyson could pick them up.

I hang up the phone and got to work on the wedding announcement for the paper, it was 2:30, when I left for lunch. I went over to the Hotdog Guy Samson, to get one of the best dogs in the city. I went to sit down on the riverfront had my lunch.

After lunch I got back to work, my phone was still buzzing, when I picked up, I saw it was from Tyson, he had left a voice mail, saying the pictures were ready for pick up.

The time had seemed to fly by after lunch, I got the column to the editor for print, and letting him know I was doing my announcement for the paper and I'll be turning it soon.

I was on my way to go get the pictures, I called Tyson and told him I was going to get the pictures and I'd see him when I got home or when he made it.

I parked the car and ran inside to get the pictures, Joshua was at the counter. I asked him would he be available for the 25th, that we could pay him if he was or did he know anyone who would be available to do my wedding.

Joshua said he would be available as long as he could be a guess at the wedding and the reception there was no charge, we considered him family since high school and he was a good friend I knew for a while.

I looked at the pictures. They were good photos, really good. Everyone looked gorgeous in their get up even the photos of Tyson and me, it was so hot, and our love melted off the page.

I sat the pictures down and went to take me a shower, I could hear Tyson's car pulling in, as I got out the shower, I ran in the bedroom and got dressed as he came the door.

"Hey baby" he called out to me as I greeted him in the kitchen doorway.

"Are you ready?" he asked.

He caught a glimpse of the photos, he picked them up and looked them over, and his was in such amazement. His face looked like a kid watching fireworks on the 4th of July.

"Damn that's us babe, and just think in 2 weeks you will be Mr. Tyson Lemont Jacks- Styles."

He looked me in my eyes, holding my hands, and kissed my lips. Once he got out the tub, went to the kitchen where he fixed us a couple of sandwiches and some chips. We sat at the table in our undies, we ate and talked.

I told him about Joshua being our wedding photographer. Tyson was cool with it after seeing the photographs earlier.

We headed to the bedroom said our prayers and got in bed. We were laying face to face, our arms wrapped around each other as we drifted off to la la land.

Chapter 19

With the wedding 1 week away, Tyson and I seemed to be very busy planning and putting the final touches on everything for our special day.

At work, I spoke to my boss, inviting him and the office to my wedding and letting him know my wedding was just in a week and that I won't be working much that week because the planning my boss was really cool with me making sure things were getting done with my wedding and that he would even take care of things with my column while I was away.

I told him I was planning to do my ad in the paper and he was cool with it, just made sure I run things by the editor, and I was so excited. I went to work, preparing things for the ad in the paper. I wanted to get it out soon as possible.

When everything was set, I called in Devon Shaw one of the editors to look at my ad. He gave me the green light. He took over things from there making sure it made to be printed.

I left the office to head out to Carter's aunt's house to discuss the menu for the reception and the budget at. At Mrs. Lea's we made our menu of Fried chicken, mashed potatoes, greens, cornbread, yams black eyed peas, ham with Pineapple slices, mac and cheese, turkey, dressing, potato salad, ribs, catfish, and the cake, to feed 50 guests, which came out to every bit of $600 dollars and $300 for her time.

We headed over to Brookshire's to get the things we needed. We then went over to the Fresh Fish Market for about 10 to 20 pounds of catfish, to make sure we had more than enough fish. Once things were done we got the food back to Mrs. Lea so she could get to work with the cooking.

When I got back to the office to check out the ad, there was a small box sitting on my desk, I closed the door to Tyson popping out at me.

"Sup Bay, your boss got in touch with me and told me how busy you were with the planning, I decided to come surprise and you since we may not have a chance to be alone until the wedding."

He picked up the box, placed it in his pocket and we headed out to the elevator. Tyson called for the limousine to meet us at curb, when we got inside there was White Roses, Champaign, and Chocolate Covered Strawberries.

We were relaxing, riding around in this limousine, just having a great time, talking and cracking jokes like old friends, when Tyson got really serious, he handed me the box that was sitting on my desk, it was a dog-tag chain necklace, with a letter T inside the half of a heart, he was wearing the other half with a J inside of his.

He said, "He had them made just for us, to keep you close to my heart and I want you to do the same." He took the chain out the box and placed it on my neck, kissing me sweetly.

We sat back riding down the road, things were done and all we had to do was wait for things to come together over the next few days. There was no talking about the wedding and just have some fun being together seemed to be what Tyson was feeling.

"Well what do you have planned for tonight?"

"Oh yeah I left this out, Carter set this up for us, here at the Horseshoe's casino."

When we pulled into the casino, they took our bags up to our room, while we took a walk around the casino taking selfies on each other phones, when the phone rings.

Speak of the devil...

"What's up Carter, thanks for the surprise, good looking out, where are you anyways, you and Lucas should swing by for a while".

"Thanks Ji', Maine I just got off work, Lucas said he would swing by the, we may come by later on, that's if y'all two not tied up," laughing in the background.

"Well hit me up, I'll text you the room number, if y'all come by, I guess Carter, we'll talk to you later."

We had dinner sitting in the buffet.

"So what do you have planned for us this evening my good sir?"

"You'll have to wait to see but trust me tonight will be great, just call this the pre-honeymoon," Tyson being dirty at the table.

"This should tide you over until the honeymoon, I'm making you wait after tonight, I'm cutting you off," He was laughing, like a fool.

"Alright not too much, we got things to do this week, we can't be lying around here like to worn out shoes Tyson," I said, trying to throw some shade back his way.

My phone rings again.

"Carter they had made out to meet us", I said to Tyson.

We paid the check and made our way the elevator in the main hall, just as the elevator doors open, Carter and Lucas stepped off, headed over to the elevators leading up to the casino suites, noticing the big bag Carter held in his hand, the room was on the 9th floor, room 9219.

Tyson opened the door to a nice suite, covered with lights that brighten the room so properly. King size bed, flat screen TV, hot-tub and a huge bathroom with a walk-in shower.

We kicked off our shoes and got comfortable, as Tyson and Carter rolled blunts for us, while Lucas and I prepared the shots.

We were drinking X-Rated and Carter and Lucas a bottle of Green Apple Cîroc. We placed the wet towel down at the door and we sat around having a good time, listening to music, chilling watching movies until 12:30 and I was feeling very good.

Carter and Lucas we're leaving, Tyson walked them to the elevator, in his rube, while I chilled in the hot-tub, Carter said,

"He would text us tomorrow."

I began to run a bath in the hot-tub, pouring some Tahitian Brazilian Body Wash, and lite some candles. I was relaxing in the tub, once the water was ready. Tyson had made his way back quickly. He was excited when he saw the tub filled, me chilling in all those bubbles, grinning cunningly.

Tyson began getting undressed.

"Take your time, I want to enjoy every moment of this," I said being his commander.

He stood there in front of me, looking me in my eyes. He took off his shirt tossing it to the floor. He unbuttoned his jeans letting them fall off his bubble ass sitting high like a hump on a camel back.

He stepped inside the hot-tub, I could feel my juices flowing and he wasn't even out of his boxers yet, as he stood before me taking off his boxers, I could the blood rush down my spine.

His piece was on the raise and every second was making me sweat bullets like I was loaded in a 22 caliber.

He made his way over to me, as we exchanged silly faces as we played around and wrestled in the tub, kissing making a slippery mess all over the bathroom floor.

After a while of the kids play, we lite some candles and placed them around the tub and got back in our places, we sat there talking and it felt so good being in his arms relaxing from all the excitement of the wedding.

That night Tyson held me so tight, this man was ready to give me the world and make me happy and I felt the same.

Chapter 20

The morning after, we seemed to be more relaxing than ever. I woke up to Tyson's strong hands rubbing warm oil down my shoulders, I laid there in peace. I could feel his kisses on my back, making my temperature rise.

"Baby you know we have the whole week of the honeymoon to enjoy each other's body but if your down hey what's up," I said sweetly.

"Oh I see you want me to play this game with you huh, the let's wait until its time, okay say that now and we will be rolling later so think long and hard about what you're saying and I do mean "Long and Hard", with his quotes I could tell he wanted it so I told him "How about a quickie?", and his face was lite up with a smile.

In an instant his nature was fully hard and we went in the mix, he picked me up and carried me over to the bathroom, he sat me up on the counter, he strapped up and slipped into my surface and we made such sweet music. He held my body close as he dove deeper inside, as I said his name silently in his ear and he repeated mine.

From the counter we sat up in the hot-tub where I got the pleasure of pleasing him, I rode his nature with such powerful energy I possessed until I could feel him at his climax.

He stood me up and leaning me against the tub and began to pound my surface, as he played with my nipples. I tightened my grip on his nature making his voice quiver and raise like Usher singing Trading Places.

I could feel my climax and I could see Tyson was in tune with me as he gave me a kiss while holding my hands, I could feel him exploding and in that moment I was overflowing in ecstasy silently screaming his name as he kissed my neck.

After our session, there was plenty of work to be done before the wedding, but we could handle that business over the phone. We cuddled up in the hot-tub as the warm bubbles filled up around us, Tyson was gently kissing and nibbling on my earlobe, I laughed at him.

> "Bay I have a bunch of surprises in stored for you tonight, I know you been busy with the wedding planning, but daddy needs his TLC."

> "I'm down for that Ty, you know that baby, and I can't wait until these I dos are done and we can show the world our love that you are the one, are you ready Ty?"

> "Mr. Styles, I'm as ready as I'll ever be, I finally finished my vows and I now I have some time alone with you. I just want to give everything to you and you only, I love you bae."

> "I love you too Ty, baby you finished your vows, I can't wait to hear them, I'm sure they are beautiful just as you are."

After we finished our soaking in the hot-tub, we got dressed and laid around in bed watching Dreamgirls on the tele. It was around 2 p.m., when a knock at the door, startled me.

I went to answer the door, it was a bottle of Moet, and Chocolate covered strawberries and tickets for the Tyrese live show that night sent up to our suite, I place them in the mini bar looking at Tyson.

> "This is what you were talking about, turning around to wake him up."

He was standing there with them as I ran over to him.

> "You got tickets to see my favorite singer, I can't believe it, you did this for me," I kissed his face.

> "Yeah I did and I wanted this look right here in your eyes," as he wiped the two tears drops falling from my eyes.

I sat the tickets on the dresser, as we lay back down in bed as we were, Tyson laid his head across my stomach, as I rubbed his head gently, watching that grin on his face.

From the bed I could see the most beautiful breathtaking view through the window. The sun was beginning to set across the clear blue sky.

I've never seen anything so perfect in my life until today, it felt as if my mother, father, and Mrs. Coco were saying they couldn't be happier in this moment for us, I swear I could see their faces across the sky, smiling and showing how much they were pleased with Tyson and I.

After a while I drifted off to la la land, where I fell into a dream of beautiful colors and lights, that were surrounding us and there was a party going on there. In the mist was Tyson with his hand out for mine, he slips the ring on my finger and I did the same, it was a sure sign we were heading in the right direction.

Then off in the distance I heard his voice, "Baby, baby, baby, get up we got dinner reservations for 6, in 30 minutes."

I got up to get dressed, Tyson dressed me and I dressed him, and finally we headed out the door. In the elevator, we shared sweet tender kisses and exchanged some jokes to pass the ride down stairs. Once we were out the elevator, we were heading to the Rock and Roll Café for dinner, were Tyson wined and dined me.

We talked and I told him what happened in the room while he was sleeping as I laid there watching the sunset across the sky, he was blown away and that wasn't all I told him about the dream, his face seemed to melt on to his hands as we waited for our meals.

Tyson had a steak and I had the lobster dinner, we had a great time just sitting there enjoying very delectable bite of this sensational meal, with a glass of Merlot and for dessert we shared a piece of Chocolate cake, tripled layered topped with whipped cream and 2 cherries.

After dinner, we headed outside just to talk a walk around the Horseshoe over to the Boardwalk looking around at all the people passing by shopping and having fun.

Tyson and I went over to the Chocolate Crocodile, we ordered Chocolate candies, paid for them, then headed back to the casino, just in time to get the tickets for the Tyrese concert.

We gave the guy our tickets, got the stubs and headed to get our seats which were right upfront to the stage. Tyrese started the show and set the mood. He moved the crowd with "Sweet Lady and sent a shout out to all the lovers with his song "One", while Tyson and I ate our chocolate and sang very badly all night long.

After the show we retired to our suite to pop the bottle of Moet, that night we laid in bed watching The Wiz eating those Chocolate covered Strawberries in our undies. After Dorothy's long journey back home, we got settled in those Silk sheets.

Tyson and I cuddled up in each other's arms, laying there looking at one another, so full of joy and stuffed from all that food we had eaten today. He kissed me goodnight and we finally fell asleep, relieved of the stress of the event soon to take place.

Chapter 21

Today was the day before wedding and it seemed to be something weird in the air, when I got up at 8 a.m. When Tyson rolled over, I was on the phone mines and his making sure thing were getting done, for a moment he laid there for a moment, admiring me, watching me take charge and it made him just laugh.

> "We're getting married tomorrow, and you're lying there laughing at me, get up we have to go, we have things to get done."

He jumped up out of bed, grabbed some clothes he had lying around. Tyson had our bags packed, and already down in the car. After he cleaned himself up and had gotten dressed, we quickly made our way downstairs and we were heading home. In the car I was still burning the phones up making sure things were getting done and things were definitely getting done.

I called Mrs. Lea, she was already in the kitchen at her house and she informed me that she would be at the house tomorrow at 12 noon.

Tyson called for our Tuxes and they had a problem with the cleaners burning our Tuxes while pressing them, leaving us with 24 hours to get Tuxes and at that point all they had were black Tuxedo suits.

Once we got to the house, to meet the decorators, who were just arriving at the house, as we pulled into the driveway.

We were greeted by the head decorator Kayla Harris as she stood their hand on her hips.

"Hi I see you're late for your own décor/rehearsal, Oh I'm Kayla Harris or just call me Mrs. Kay, she added.

We opened the door and Kayla was impressed with the house, and the space in the house.

"You have a nice home here darling child, oh yesssss darling we can definitely work with this space here," she said.

We had enough room to set up chairs around the house and the reception would be held in the Ballroom at the Hilton. Tyson told me to he was going to take care of the tuxes, while I helped with the decorations here at the house.

Tyson left in his car, on his way to get Carter and Rico to let them know the situation on the tuxedos and he told them they had things under control.

Carter said he would meet them there. Tyson went to the shop about the situation with the tuxedos, he had everybody's sizes, and they already knew why they were there when the guys came at 12 noon.

He got the new tuxes for us and they were on their way out and I had forgotten to book the limo so Tyson had to do something quick when Carter said to Tyson.

"My cousin Joey owes me a favor, your limo will be there, trust me on that my bro, my gift to you guys from me, plus that one less thing to stress over."

Back at the house, Tyson called me about the tuxes. I called Brittney to see was she getting herself together, and she was as I reminded her to get her some rest for the dress rehearsal tonight at 6 and not to be late.

I left the house to go get me a haircut before the dinner, cruising listening to Mario "Cryin" on the radio, when I thought about it Tyson and I didn't have a song for our 1st dance as a married couple, when the phone begins to ring it was Jeffery.

"Hello yeah this is Jisain"

"Hey Maine this is Jeffery tell me something, do you think you're going to do this tomorrow, and marry Tyson?"

"He's not me, he doesn't love you like I did, he doesn't please you like I did, make you bite your lips like I did, touch you the way I did, treat you the way I did."

"That's right exactly like you said Did as in you don't anymore, you don't think I love him but I do, I know he loves me more than life itself. He's showed me real true love, sincere and honest love.

He wouldn't hurt me the way you did. He's making me his life partner for the rest of his, our lives and you have will have nothing to do with that.

I'll tell you this as well, there's one thing he did you never did he made us everything. I'll be proud to be at his side until death does us apart.

Why did you call, to get your blues together, why you aren't with Khadijah anyway, oh don't tell me she left your ass too.

What do we call this in the world karma, she's a bitch huh, and you know what you had coming, but I'll do this for you to come to our reception at the Hilton in the ballroom.

I think I have someone for you, the two of you would be good together, it starts at 4:30," I added just as I ended the call.

When I got back to the house Tyson was pulling up, we waked in to see the house was beautiful.

The yard was covered in Orchids, there was a fountain flowing with water and there were white lilies and roses floating in the fountain, the house was covered on orchids and lined up across the floor, chairs were everywhere, and a table for gifts.

The aisle had a red carpet laid down to walk, with ribbon lining the back of the chairs with baby blue, black and white balloons.

Over at the ballroom, they were setting up the space for the reception and the D.J. everything was so beautiful.

"Baby this place is gorgeous, and everything looks so good, how did we afford this this stuff?"

"Good news I just found out your girl Kayla, is my cousin through my mom's like right after you left, we talked and her dad and my mom are 1st cousins, so she's charging us a player price of about $2000 for the work here and for the ballroom at the hotel.

She pulled some strings and we don't have to pay for anything," Tyson answered.

"Oh okay well think you, darling cousin in law," I said.

"Oh yeah darling, it was nothing when you find a relative. God has blessed today, so now I am blessing you and my cousin here.

Just promise me 2 things you that my husband Dexter and our baby girl Camille to come to your wedding and send us pictures from the honeymoon," Kayla asked.

"You have my word and your family is also welcomed to our wedding. I welcome you guys into our house and our lives, thank you so much for all you've done today," I said.

Around 5:30 I called the wedding party to do the dress rehearsal. While they were in route, I got to talking Tyson and asking him what was on our wedding song.

Tyson looked at me, "Oh yeah baby I know the perfect song," he took me took me to his mama's old albums and pulled up a Luther Vandross album, with the song Here and Now.

We sat down and started the song as we listened I could see Tyson staring into my eyes, he was so ready and I knew that song was perfect.

"Baby this is our song, and I had the idea of this song and you walking down the aisle to me," Tyson said.

"YES," I answered kissing him on his bottom lip.

The gang had arrived at 6:10 and we got to business.

"Here we go."

"Rico, you'll follow Brittney as drop the flower petals, you'll have the rings, so please be careful," I said, giving them directions.

"Carter, you and Lucy will be walking down behind them, Tyson, baby you'll be there at this spot here waiting for me and I'll be right behind these two, are we ready, you all have your assignment plain and simple, the coordinator will be watching us as we run through the rehearsal."

It took a moment for us because Luther made all the ladies cry during the rehearsal. After two hours we finally had the steps in place.

Kayla called her husband Dexter and gave him the news, to come meet the family so we could all get acquainted.

We were all sitting around the house chilling and Tyson went to the stash box and brought over some herbal tea for us, little did we know Lucas was on his way, with some herb of his own.

While we were sitting around enjoying each other's company Kayla asked?

"Was this bachelor's party"?

I looked at Tyson looking back at me, "Yeah! Yes, it is well let's party," we said together.

We turned up the music and began dancing, we were having a great time, just as Lucas and Michael walked in the middle of our progress and fell in the line, blunts were everywhere and we were so happy and excited tonight.

My ever clever Tyson went to get the camcorder and began filming the highlights of the evening.

Kayla finally got a chance to introduce us to her husband Michael, she got his attention.

"Cuzo this is my baby Dexter, Dex met my cousin Tyson," and they hit it off instantly.

Tyson introduced me to Dexter, "Bae come meet my cousin in law Dexter."

When I walked over, Dexter seemed to be surprised to see Tyson grab my hand in his then kissed it.

"Were getting married tomorrow, we welcome you to the party," Tyson said.

"Cool where can I roll this up?" Dexter asked, taking a bag of loud from his pocket.

"Shit right where you standing, I answered, our house is yours make yourself at home," I answered making sure Dexter felt right home with the gang.

We went to the kitchen to make some snacks Mini Tacos, enchiladas, tamales, rotail dip for the guests and some leftover Pound cake.

We played a drinking game and some dominoes until 10:30. The gang then split us up leaving me at the house with my sis Lucy, my girl Lena, Brittney, Lucas, and Kayla.

Tyson, Dexter, Rico, LaDorian, and Carter were going to get together at Carter's house and they would stay there the reminder of the night after they left from the bar having drinks.

We cleaned the house quickly, got a shower and got in bed. Tyson was texting me but the girls had taking my phone.

"No contact until the wedding, its bad luck."

I didn't have any jitters at all. Tyson had found another family member and the house was blessed with everyone's love, laughter and friendship, God really had blessed us that night and tomorrow was just as big as today.

The next morning 9:30 am, I got in the kitchen to fix a huge breakfast for everyone. When the gang came in the kitchen they were greeted.

"Good morning, I did this for you all, to show our gratitude for everything you guys have done for Tyson and me."

Lucy return my phone to me finally I had a chance to see my messages from Tyson, he was so excited and he knew I couldn't reply to the messages, I told him Lucy had my phone and I couldn't have contact with him until he got back to the house for the wedding.

"Who's going to bless the meal?"

"How about me," said Lena?

"Join hands everyone.

Dear Lord,

We come to you this morning, 1st thanking you for this day, for waking us up and for watching over us all night long, for friends and family to share in Tyson and Jisain's special day designed in your grace that is soon to take place.

For this meal that has been prepared for our natural health, to give you blessings in Jesus name we pray,

We all say Amen."

After our breakfast, we left for the house under the charge of the cleaning crew, whom came to make sure the house was just right, while we got ready for the wedding.

I went to meet Mrs. Lea and help to set up the food for reception at the hotel. My phone seemed to be ringing off the hook and it was beginning to drive me crazy, because people didn't know what time the wedding started from the invitations.

 Everyone seemed to want to know what time to meet at the house, where the house was located or who was all invited and all that jazz. Lucy and Lena took over my phone at that point telling me.

"Jisain you stay calm and go get yourself together for the wedding."

I was so nervous, the guests were beginning to arrive and I hadn't seen Tyson all that day. I went and filled the tub for a soak before I got dressed. Lucy finally returned my phone just so I could text Tyson to make sure he was okay and that he wasn't freaking out like I was and he was.

At 2:30 I was finally getting dressed just before we were lining up to began the ceremony.

As we were lining up Lucy said she had the perfect song for us all to walk down the aisle and they already had the music changed, before I could change my mind.

Brittney was dressed in a dazzling white dress with a big Pink bow, with her pearls and white heels, her hair was pinned up in huge curls, and she was a gorgeous flower girl.

Rico wore his black tux so handsomely with our rings on top of the little with pillow. Carter and Lucas were sharp in their places.

The music began to play and it was Beyoncé and Luther Vandross's "the Closer I Get to You", Lucy and myself making our way into the room down the aisle.

Tears begin streaming down my face as I looked at Tyson standing there smiling at us so sweetly, looking so damn good I began smiling back at him, as I saw the flash from Joshua's camera filming us taking our soft rehearsed steps. Pastor Parker was dazzled by the scene taking place.

When I had finally made my way to Tyson, we stood their hand in hand before Pastor Parker began reading from the bible on the occasion of weddings and blessed us with a prayer.

He said that we had prepared our vows that we would be sharing with one another and everyone assembled.

I read mines 1st.

"Tyson that night I met you, I never thought that you be here waiting for me, to complete this half of a man and make me whole at last.

You've helped to heal my aching heart. You filled my life with a joy I never knew. You love me whole heartedly and you came to carry me with you to our ever after, with nothing but laughter and joy.

I promise to devote my heart to you only. I vow to share all I have to remind you that we are one, I love you baby."

Tyson then read his vows.

"Jisain, baby I love you, you've showed me real, true and honest love. You came into my life and changed this spoiled lil boy into the proud man that stands here today.

You saw a fragile, loving, and kind man underneath the rough act I give to the world. I vow to stand by you, each day in and out, through everything that comes our way.

Give you more love could imagine. Fill your rainy days with sunshine and flowers and keep you close to my heart.

With God's grace, I'll love you forever more babe", he was so kind and loving, as I wiped the tears from his sincere face.

Pastor Parker asked, "Who had the rings?"

Rico placed them in his hand, giving me the 1st ring to place on Tyson's finger he said to repeat these words.

"I take you as my life partner, with this ring I seal my commitment to you before God to death do us part."

"I Jisain take you Tyson as my life partner, with this ring I seal my commitment to you before God to death do us part," as tears ran down my face.

"I Tyson take you Jisain, to be my life partner, with this ring I seal my commitment to you before God to death do us part."

"Now before God and your witnesses here I pronounce you Husband and Husband, sealed with a kiss."

That kiss seemed to stop time, it was passionate yet sweet and after our kiss, we turned to face our guests.

"It is my honor to announce to the world Mr. and Mr. Tyson Styles-Jacks."

Lucy had the broom already placed for us to jump, as we walked back up the aisle, I swear I felt my world fill with fireworks, my dream had finally come true in one moment. Our family and friends were standing all around cheering for us as the rice flew.

I heard Tyson whispering to me,

"Now we are complete you and me nothing or no one can stop us now."

After the rice had been thrown, we all gathered out in front of the house for a big family photo. Tyson and I in front, Carter and Lucas to our left with his aunt Lea. Rico and Brittney, Lucy, LaDorian and Leah, Kinsten and Brittney's parents all gathered around us.

After the pictures had been taking, we rushed to the limo to head over to the hotel for the reception, in the car Tyson looked at me asking?

"Hey Mr. Jisain Jacks how does that sound?"

"That sounds like bells to my ears."

When we got to the hotel's reception hall, everyone we could think of was there. When we walked in the reception doors everyone stood around cheering, clapping, and cheering to see us as newlyweds.

We walked over to our table. We had things all set up for our guests. We ate dinner and laughed talking for hours, in the middle of dinner Carter stood to do a toast, as she tapped his glass with his spoon, we gave him the floor.

"To my new friends Jisain and Tyson, I've watched you two for some time and I see the way you two look at other and it's so obvious that Jisain you love Tyson.

Tyson I've never seen Ji so happy from the way he talks about and would never shut up. So I send this toast up to you Jisain and Tyson you've found your good thing, may you and Tyson be blessed on this newly formed path and I'll do all I can to keep you two in check, I love y'all, congratulation here, here."

As we sipped the Cristal down, Tyson took my hand, I stood there just blushing and gushing in pure joy and happiness.

"To everyone here this evening, we would like to thank you all for being part ceremony this afternoon, to help us celebrate our love tonight," he said.

"To everyone here I would like you all to know that this is happiest day of my life. I am so honored to be standing beside this heavenly gift I am blessed to open for the rest of my life.

I thank you so much for coming my rescue, so I toast to you my Tyson, my hero, I love you baby."

As I made my toast Tristian came with a nice box wrapped in blue wrapping paper.

"Tyson, Jisain, I didn't want to be a bad wolf so congrats, I'll be out of here in a minute."

"No your welcome to stay, there's plenty of food and drinks have a great time."

Jeffery and a guy friend came in, he handed Tyson a card with our names on it. We sat the gifts on the table to go and share our first dance as a married couple.

The spotlight was casting a shadow on us as we stood in the center of the room Tyson holding me close enough to smell my Hummer cologne that I had brought just a few weeks ago.

As we danced to Luther's "Here and Now", we exchanged whispers in each other ear saying "I love you" and soon after our dance went to cut the wedding cake. We thanked our guests for coming out again before we left for the night.

When we got home we were so tired, we just fell asleep in our tuxes lying, face to face.

Chapter 22

After such a long and joyous day yesterday, Tyson and I were up getting pack for our honeymoon cruise. Tyson did the bag packing while I cooked us some breakfast.

While we were busy, my phone begins to ring, it was Carter, he had proposal, and we couldn't refuse or that it could be a favor if we choose that he'd be over to talk to us when he got a chance.

We had a few hours to kill before we had to catch the train to New Orleans, I told him, and that we'd meet him and Lucas for lunch, over at Ihop.

Once Tyson had a chance to get things packed, I was scrambling the eggs, Tyson was packing the limousine.

"We should be leaving out for the train around 4, to be checked into our hotel suite by 9 o'clock 10 at the latest."

"Well that's cool we just have meet Carter for lunch before we leave out, so save room for lunch."

"Oh and babe, I got to run to see Lil' Rico, he's leaving for the tournament with the basketball team tonight in Huston."

Tyson went through the house, checking the window and the doors, making sure things were locked down tight and secured. I checked the plugs for any hazards. I went into the bedroom and grabbed the camera from the dresser.

We were ready to go, after we took a shower and got dressed. Once we were safely inside the limousine, I gave the driver the directions for the G.P.S. system. We sat back to enjoy the ride.

Tyson insisted on a message, so I told him to take his shirt off, I went to work, he was telling me that he was ready to get me alone in that room on that boat.

"Oh so what do you plan to do on that boat, while I'm fighting sea sickness," I said laughing.

"You'll have to wait and see, damn babe rub just a little bit lower," he said.

As I rubbed his lower back, he was melting from my hands of ecstasy, I could hear him ooh and awing, so I kissed his shoulder, breaking his attention.

"Oh okay, you want some huh?"

"Oh no babe, you're waiting to that boats in motion, I want to enjoy that hot ass body."

We pulled up to Rico and Kinsten's house, Tyson got his shirt on and we made our way to the door. Tyson ring the doorbell, the door opened and there was Rico still half asleep.

"Y'all should be cruising on the Gulf of Mexico?" in a Jamaican accent

"Yeah we leaving later, just came bye to wish you luck in Houston lil' man and I want you to have something for you Mama would to have this," it was a locket. It had pictures of Mother Coco and Rico.

Tyson placed the locket in his hand.

"Hey I love you Rico and I wanted you think about come staying with us for a lil while, talk to your Pops and we'll iron out the rest," he added.

"Tyson you know we have to keep on schedule to keep, Rico good luck lil' man, call us with good news," I was giving him the head nod.

We all walked back to the limo, when we were inside, Rico closed the door behind us, and Tyson stood up in the sun roof shouting.

"Good luck Lil' Rico."

I could hear Rico shouting back.

"Enjoy the honeymoon!!!!!!"

Back in the car, I was calling Lucy to check on her before we went sailing away, her phone went to voicemail, she was probably sleeping from all the partying last night, so I left her a voicemail telling her I loved her and I'd be expecting a call from you every day, while I'm out at sea.

It was around 2:30 when I got the call from Carter, they were heading to Ihop, at the same time as we were, I asked him to hold us table, and letting him know we'd be there soon.

When we got to Ihop, Carter and Lucas were holding us a booth. We sat down and looked over the menu. We ordered our drinks and waited to order our meals.

"So what's this news, y'all got us here," Me all anxious, for the news?

"Well we know y'all are leaving out today, the honeymoon is for the week and the house will be alone, Lucas and I were wondering if we could house sit for you?" Carter asked.

"Hey it's cool with me, what you think Jisain?" Tyson asked.

"Yeah it's cool with me I'm just waiting to get under this man right here."

"Just hold down the fort, y'all please take care of mom's" and Tyson's face went blank when he realized it was our house and he smiled.

We ordered burgers and fries.

While the burgers were grilling, Carter said.

"Lucas and I pitched in and got this for you guys, congrats again," it was an envelope with a card, the card had grooms cutting the cake, when I opened it $250 dollars fell out and the card.

Tyson and I burst out laughing.

"Thank you so much you guys."

"So Lucas, what's up man, did you have a great time last night," Tyson asked.

"Yeah, I had a great time especially when Carter and I walked down the aisle, it was something, in a dream."

"So we have to pack for the week and these two should be on the road, and y'all go ahead we'll get this here handled," Carter said.

We walked outside Carter got the keys from Tyson and they exchanged information among each other as we got into the limousine.

Our reservations are at Marriott Hotel and Suites for the next 2 days and then we would leave out to see Sunday morning.

We were in the limousine, and the ride was long ahead. I laid there in Tyson's arms, I was imagining what the room would be like, the beautiful things that we would see, and I could see that my life had finally came full circle in that moment.

As we rode along down I-20 to Alexandria, I could hear our wedding song playing on the radio. I looked into Tyson's eyes.

I could feel my heart melting away like cool lemonade in the middle of sunny July.

Tyson whispered, "Here's to forever" in my ear.

We laid there watching the clouds roll by, it seemed the cruise and the honeymoon had already started, as the time ticked away.

Coming Soon:

Coming Full Circle 2: Marriage Money and Mayhem

The Confessions of Conceited Drama King Collection

Check me out online

@Facebook.Com/ Jerrick Thomas

@Instagram.Com/ Jerrick Thomas

@Twitter.Com/ Jerrick Thomas

Hey y'all check out this exclusive content from Coming Full Circle 2: Marriage, Money and Money. I hope you guys enjoy.

Peace and Blessings,

Jrayis Deyond

Dear Jisain,

Sorry to leave this note on your car, this is Lena, I decided to leave town, quietly and secretly to avoid any more physical abuse from Jamie James I'm heading out now and I'll call you when I figure things out where I'll be.

Don't try to call me I've changed my number as part of the situation, I'll call you my brother, Kenny's with me and he told me to tell you thank you for being there at the house that day. It made feel safe knowing his uncle came the rescue and I am too.

I'll talk to you soon,

You're Bestie/Sister Lena.

P.S. Wait until you find out who Jeffery is seeing now lol.

I folded the note back up placing it in my pocket.

I went to working on the column and I did a PSA.

Hey You Guys,

In today's column I wanted to talk about domestic violence. It happens to all us, yeah the men too people. The point I'm getting at is simply this. Love doesn't hurt and if someone is expressing that type of love you should get away from them fast. I've witnessed this from a dear friend of mine who she just left her hometown here due to this situation and it was horrible to see her in that condition. I was truly happy to be there and help her after that scene had diffused.

 My heart cries for anyone and everyone who has ever experienced this type of love and trust me it's not worth your life. If you are in this type of situation you should do everything you can in your power to get away from that today. Get the resources you need or call someone who can help you if you go through something like this have a support system.

Remember love doesn't hurt and staying with someone who beats you for affection is no better living in a pit of snakes.

Signed,

Mr. Styles-Jacks

52356661R00086

Made in the USA
Middletown, DE
09 July 2019